THUNDER IN THE MORNING

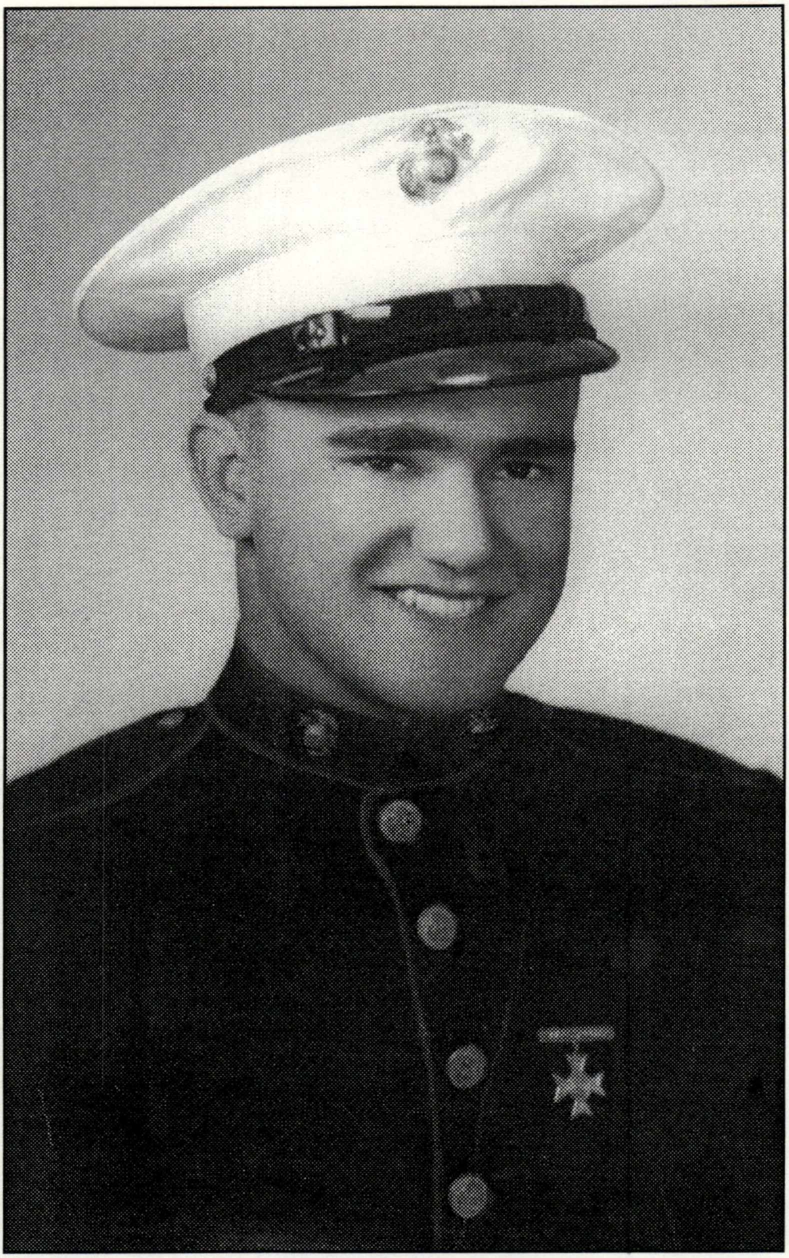

THUNDER IN THE MORNING

A WORLD WAR II MEMOIR

by

HOMER H. GRANTHAM

With a Foreword by Charles Edward Jackson

PHOENIX INTERNATIONAL, INC.
2003

Copyright © 2003 by Homer H. Grantham

All rights reserved
Printed in the United States

06 05 04 03   4 3 2 1

Designed by John Coghlan

No part of this publication may be reproduced, stored in a retrieval system, or transmitted in any form or by any means—electronic, mechanical, photocopy, recording, or any other—except for brief quotations in printed reviews, without the prior permission of the publisher.

Inquiries should be addressed to:

Phoenix International, Inc.
1501 Stubblefield Road
Fayetteville, Arkansas 72703
Phone (479) 521-2204
www.phoenixbase.com

Title page image and cover image of the USS *Idaho* courtesy of the National Archives
Frontispiece: Homer H. Grantham, 1944

Library of Congress Cataloging-in-Publication Data

Grantham, Homer H., 1925–
    Thunder in the morning : a World War II memoir / by Homer H. Grantham ; with a foreword by Charles Edward Jackson.
    p. cm.
    Includes bibliographical references.
    ISBN 0-9713470-4-2
    1. Grantham, Homer H., 1925– 2. United States. Marine Corps. Marine Division, 1st—History. 3. World War, 1939–1945—Regimental histories—United States. 4. World War, 1939–1945—Personal narratives, American. 5. World War, 1939–1945—Campaigns—Pacific Area. 6. Marines—United States—Biography. I. Title.

D769.37 1st .G73 A3 2003
940.54'8173—dc22

2003062323

CONTENTS

Foreword, by Charles Edward Jackson   vii

Introduction   ix

Chapter 1   Thunder in the Morning   1

Chapter 2   Pavuvu and the First Marine Division   56

Chapter 3   Okinawa: The Last Battle   63

Chapter 4   China Duty   106

Epilogue   127

Appendix   131

Bibliography   139

The USS *Pennsylvania,* August 1, 1943, near Puget Sound after a refit.

FOREWORD

Six thousand miles away and fifty-seven years ago Homer Grantham and I played two distinct but highly coordinated parts in the Pacific war against the Japanese at the Battle of Peleliu. As narrated in *Thunder in the Morning* the nineteen-year-old Homer was a U.S. Marine private in the First Marine Division that made an amphibious assault and landing on that Japanese-held island. I was a twenty-seven-year-old navy lieutenant on the battleship *Pennsylvania,* a part of an armada of ships that made up the Peleliu Bombardment and Fire Support Group. In his book Homer relates in a masterly fashion the critical role of his Fourth Marine Joint Assault Signal Company. These men landed in one of the first waves to hit the beach. As they advanced inland against the enemy, they maintained communication with the navy ships and gave us directions as to the targets to hit. I was an officer in charge of one of the *Pennsylvania's* four gun turrets equipped with four 14-inch guns that responded to their skilled directives. For three days prior to the landing we bombarded Japanese installations on the island. The object was the complete destruction of known targets.

On the morning of September 15, 1944, the troops made their first landing. As those brave marines pushed forward, sustaining heavy casualties, naval guns continued to support, principally with our smaller five-inch guns. I leave to Private Grantham the story of the eventual victory despite the heaviest losses that I had seen in five previous amphibious operations in which my ship had participated.

After this battle my ship was a part of the navy fleet in a

traditional surface engagement in the Battle of Surigao Strait south of Leyte in the Philippines in which the Japanese lost two battleships and three destroyers.

After that engagement I was assigned to the U.S. Army as a naval gunfire liaison officer training army personnel in a Joint Assault Signal Company, a mirror image of the structure in which Homer was a part with the marines.

This operation came to a halt when the A-bomb was dropped on Hiroshima. An almost certainly near scenario to develop would have been that Homer and I would have been brought together again in the planned invasion of Japan. But the two boys' paths did not cross again from the time of the 1944 Battle of Peleliu until our unexpected meeting in June of 2002 at a Drew County Historical Society meeting in Monticello, Arkansas, where we both lived at the time.

I am honored to have been asked by this brave marine to relate how so long ago we shared this memorable experience.

       Charles Edward Jackson
       Lieutenant U.S.N.R., Ret.

INTRODUCTION

I had never intended to write about my marine experience until I moved to Monticello, Arkansas, in December of 1998. My son, Craig, had taken a course that had some history of World War II, and he asked me to write about my experience as a marine in that war. After agonizing about it some, I decided to put down on paper the events as I remember them from November 12, 1943, till March 29, 1946.

Several books have been written about the Peleliu and Okinawa battles in which the First Marine Division participated. The First Marine Division stopped the Japanese at Guadalcanal. Their next engagement was at Cape Glouster, then on to Peleliu and Okinawa. My story picks up with the assault on Peleliu and continues on to the battle for Okinawa and then on to northern China until I returned back to the United States at San Diego, California.

In all the books I have read about the Peleliu and Okinawa battles not much was said about the role of the naval gunfire spotting parties who directed the naval bombardment after the troops had landed. My story is about the battles as seen through the eyes of one of the spotting team marines. In the Peleliu campaign my outfit was listed as the Fourth Joint Assault Signal Company (JASCO). For the Okinawa campaign we were organized as the First Assault Signal Company (ASCO).

It was only by a quirk of fate that Lieutenant Jackson wrote the Foreword. I was trying to get Major Jonas M. Platt, who is in the story, to do the Introduction, but sadly he passed away in August of 2000. I met Lieutenant Charles E. Jackson at a meeting of the Drew County Historical Society in Monticello, Arkansas, in June of 2002. The battleship *Pennsylvania,* which was Charles Jackson's ship, was the one that blew holes in the four-foot-thick walls of the blockhouse that had been holding up the advance of the First Battalion of the First Marine Regiment on the third day of that battle, destroying it and killing twenty Japanese in it from the concussion. After this the Second Battalion quickly knocked out the surrounding pillboxes and continued their advance. The Second Battalion of the First Marine Regiment had the right flank, the Third Battalion, which my party was attached to, had the left flank, while the First Battalion was in the center on the third day of the Peleliu campaign. These three battalions were the infantry for the First Marine Regiment of which the other First Division Marine Regiments were the Fifth Marines, the Seventh Marines, and the Eleventh Artillery Regiment.

I had many friends in our assault signal company that I would have liked to have mentioned. My story hinges around my particular six-man spotting team with a few exceptions. My marine experience was burned into my mind. I still dream about it sometimes, but not as much as in the earlier years afterward. Time has filtered out some of the memories, but as written in this book the main experiences are still with me. The appendix tells the part that the Fifth and Seventh Marine Regiments, the Eleventh Artillery Regiment, and the Eighty-first Army played in finishing the battle.

THUNDER IN THE MORNING

1

THUNDER IN THE MORNING

It was September of 1942, ninety-seven degrees in the shade, and the first high school football game of the eastern Arkansas season. Across from me was West Helena's all-conference right guard, all one hundred seventy pounds of him. And there was me, Marvell's left guard at one hundred thirty pounds. And if my light weight wasn't enough to undermine my confidence, there were the cleats on my shoes. They were about worn off. Neither Marvell High School's budget nor mine could afford a new pair.

West Helena had the ball. The second their center snapped the ball, I submarined between the big guy's legs and tackled the halfback. Several plays and bruises later, we took possession of the ball without the bigger team scoring. Our first play was a sweep around the right end. When the ball was snapped, I attempted to block West Helena's gorilla guard. He shoved me aside. I swung my legs around and caught him just above the ankles. He fell flat on his face. I was surprised and pleased to hear his grunt of disgust as he shook off the dust. Being so thin turned to my advantage. It was easy for me to turn sideways and scoot through West Helena's large line. I worried and harassed the big guard for two quarters.

We held the West Helena team to just one touchdown as the half ended. However, the heat began to sap our strength. Marvell was a small school and most of our team had to double up on both defense and offense, giving them no rest breaks. A third of the team was too exhausted to come out for the second half. Our sophomore substitutes were small and inexperienced. The manager, an older student, decided to move me from the line to the backfield. I had no experience playing halfback but I agreed to give it my best.

West Helena kicked off to start the second half. The ball sailed toward me where I picked it up near the right sideline. I started up the field along the sideline. At the fifty-yard line were all our cheerleaders. West Helena seemed to hesitate at the fifty-yard line, thinking I would cut over toward the opposite side. This forced me to decide whether to stay in bounds or to plow into the cheerleaders. I drove hard smack into the West Helena defense gathered there. A big cheer went up as I picked myself up off the grass. I heard the referee say, "Son, that's bringing the ball on up the field." He knew we were badly out-manned and out-sized. And we were exhausted.

West Helena beat us thirty to nothing, but it was a game that I will always remember. I learned two lessons that hot September day in 1942. It takes trained personnel with good equipment to win a battle on whatever field of endeavor you are in. And it doesn't hurt to have some cheerleaders on the sideline.

Two years later, on another hot September day, I was again wearing a uniform, but this time it had a steel helmet with a camouflaged cover. A light carbine was slung over my shoulder. The immense difference between the intensity on Marvell High's football field and this field of battle was staggering.

I was part of a six-man naval gunfire spotting team riding in an amphibious tractor in the third assault wave. The tractor was crawling up a sandy beach at Peleliu in the South Pacific, five hundred miles east of the Philippine Islands. As the tractor crawled farther in, I began to hear the most nerve-shattering noise I had ever heard. The air cracked around me with rifle and machine-gun fire, along with mortar fire. When the driver stopped the tractor, he and his assistant got on the two front-mounted .50-caliber machine guns and began firing over the heads of the first two waves. Their target was a small hill in the distance. As soon as the tractor stopped we began to scramble out over the side, taking with us all our radio gear. I had just handed the antenna bag to one of the fellows when the driver yelled, "Hurry up, we've got to get out of here and pick up more men." I was a little slow getting out because I wanted to make sure we had all the equipment we needed. Maybe I was subconsciously thinking about the lack of good football shoes that cost us so many games.

When all the gear was out, the driver threw the tractor in reverse. He was already backing up as I jumped down to the sandy beach of Peleliu. Monk, our lieutenant, was just ahead, motioning us forward. He crouched to present as small a target as possible, and the rest of us crouched down low, following his lead.

Around us were the ragged remains of palm trees shot away by the earlier naval shore bombardment. I could not believe I was in this situation. In high school I had followed the war from 1939 to 1943, but this was different from reading about it. Things were not what I expected. I had never been this scared in my life. A thousand thoughts passed through my mind, but there was one thought I could not shake. I could get killed.

■ ■ ■

This story is not intended to be a complete history of the battles of Peleliu and Okinawa. It is rather an account of a small six-man team that participated in these two hard-fought campaigns. Our job was to spot and call down fire support from the navy ships off shore until the tanks and artillery could be brought into play.

Our lieutenant acted as the spotter. The lieutenant was supported by a scout, whose job was to protect him. The remainder of the team were two radiomen and two telephone men, who provided communications between the spotter and the ships. Most of the time the ship was a destroyer, but at times cruisers or even battleships were used to deliver the bombardment.

Marines, soldiers, and sailors come from all different backgrounds and have distinct personalities. My background was the eastern Arkansas delta near the towns of Parkin and Marvell. I was born seven miles south of Parkin. I was the firstborn of Robert Young Grantham (nicknamed Watts) and Carrie Mae (maiden name Varner). I had a brother who was two years younger than I. He was followed by three sisters.

My dad did not own any land but farmed as a renter. He did, however, own his own mules and plow tools. Cotton was the main money crop, and at that time this area had some of the best land in the country for growing it. By the time I was seven I was helping with the cotton chopping and picking.

Half of my schooling was spent in one-room schoolhouses with only one teacher taking care of the first through eighth grades. Some places we lived made it necessary for us to walk up to two miles over dirt roads to school.

In December of 1934, we moved to the Marvell area, where my dad farmed some land owned by my mother's father.

The following summer I was ten years old. It was the best summer of my life. During the high water season, I learned to swim in the sloughs that crisscrossed the land. My grandfather had three sons: Elworth, also ten years old; Harvey, twelve years old; and Grady, fourteen. We did about everything together, from stealing watermelons to stealing June apples.

Harvey was a cheerful and enthusiastic kid. I liked him the best. He died that December from malaria. He caught it in the swampy mosquito-infested sloughs where we had spent so much time swimming, fishing, and catching turtles. It was a sad and bitter irony that those cypress-filled sloughs that gave us so much fun would play a part in Harvey's death. Though he was actually my uncle, he was more of a cousin, or even a brother, to me.

Later Grady went off to the Civilian Conservation Camp and eventually joined the army and went to Alaska, where he died from appendicitis. We were told that he held on, hoping to come home on a furlough, but apparently his appendix had burst. He never recovered. These two losses were my first experiences with grief. Harvey and Grady are both buried in a small community graveyard three miles south of where we had such a great time that summer in 1935.

Elworth was drafted into the army. I was lucky enough to go on liberty with him twice while I was at the marine base in San Diego, California, in 1944.

My dad moved our family around till 1939 when we settled on eighty acres that he rented through my mother's family. That year I started to high school, having finished the eighth grade at the local Midway grade school. At that time and in that area few of the rural kids north of Marvell went to high school. There were no buses, so I rode one of our horses to school. Mr. and Mrs. Beasley, friends of our family who lived in town, had a stable and let me keep the horse there. I spent part of my lunch hour feeding and watering my horse.

The Marvell High School had excellent teachers. The principal was H. G. Bunn. He had been at Marvell for fifteen years and was tough when it came to discipline. Most of the kids were afraid of him, including me. He knew where he stood on issues and would not be bullied by either parents or the school board. I once saw him grab a misbehaving boy by the hair and push him down in the seat. His words and actions sent a message: Behave.

While my grades were only average, I did manage to read one or two library books a week. We had no electricity so I had to read by kerosene lamps. I kept up with the war, which was just getting underway in Europe, by reading the newspaper and *Newsweek* magazine. I went out for football my sophomore year but did not play much until my senior year. Our football coach had left for the army my senior year. The boys had a lot of drive and didn't want to give up the team. The principle respected that and let us work out our own plays. Henry Thomason, one of the older students, acted as manager.

Some of the smaller schools did not even have a football team that year due to a lack of coaches and players. Statewide, a large number of seniors had volunteered for the navy. This left us playing mostly larger schools. We did not win any games, but a couple of the big schools only beat us by one touchdown. If I could have had a good pair of shoes or even shoes that had decent cleats, I believe we would have won at least one game. With a coach I believe we would have won half or more of our games. If two more seniors had been recruited, we would have beaten all but Helena and West Helena.

Our best play was a quarterback sneak between the center and me, the left guard. Another good play was with me leading interference over right tackle. Our passing wasn't too bad, either, but I did need to improve my blocking. In spite of all the obstacles to our team, I enjoyed playing football. It taught me teamwork and the value of friendship. And I liked making hard-hitting tackles.

In the following spring of 1943, I tried to enlist in the U.S. Naval Air Corps as a pilot trainee. I did not pass because I was slightly nearsighted. After graduating in June, I wanted to join the regular navy. Dad talked me out of it, asking me to wait to be drafted. My eighteenth birthday was August 15. I was drafted on November 3. In those days you could ask for the service you wanted . . . and sometimes they'd give it to you. I requested the marines.

The marines had just started taking draftees. I was the first one taken that day even though I weighed only one hundred and thirty pounds. When I got back home my dad was distressed that I had been placed in the marines. It took a lot of talking to calm him down.

A week later my dad and my uncle drove me down to Walnut Corner to catch the bus for Little Rock, Arkansas. When I got on it, I looked out the window and saw Dad wipe away a tear. It would be two and a half years before I would see him again.

I was inducted into the marines on November 12, 1943, at Little Rock, and was immediately placed in charge of twelve other recruits. We had a tiring five-day trip by steam-driven train to the marine base in San Diego, California.

Marines had only seven weeks of basic training in those days. We spent the first three weeks learning to march, run obstacle courses, make up bunks properly, and clean our rifles, and adapting to other military disciplines. Following that, we were off to spend three weeks on the rifle range to learn to shoot the eight-round clip .30-caliber M1 Garand rifle.

The rifle instructor started by showing us the different positions used to fire the rifle: standing, kneeling, sitting, and prone. I thought I'd never even come close to handling the rifle like the instructor. In three weeks we were almost as good as he was.

At the end of the rifle range training we fired for our final record. We had to get off sixteen rounds in one minute. This meant firing one eight-round clip, changing to a new eight-round clip, then firing it before the minute was up. If you did not get off all your rounds, tough luck.

During training I usually had fired sixteen rounds in forty-five seconds. For the record we fired at 200, 300, and 500 yards. I let some rounds get away in the kneeling position at 300 yards and made only one bullseye at 500 yards. I just got in the outer rings of the target at 500 yards since I was slightly nearsighted. My total score was 296, making Sharpshooter. It took 305 to make Expert. I remember one Arkansas boy making Expert. I was proud all the Arkansas boys qualified even though some only made Marksman, the lowest rating to qualify for the rifle.

After marksmanship training we went back to the marine base at San Diego to finish basic training. This included bayonet training and more obstacle courses, along with some refinement on our marching and drilling. I moved into a different twenty-man hut because I had some trouble with several fellows while training at the rifle range. It was nothing serious and now seems almost funny.

One of my fellow Arkansans liked to sing hillbilly songs. After getting back from the rifle range, he and I would sing while the other fellows would play cards. One day my buddy was singing by himself while the others were concentrating on a hot game of poker. Certain hillbilly tunes have a way of interfering with concentration, especially if you're not from Arkansas. They stopped the game long enough to tell him to shut up. Taking umbrage with this treatment of my friend, I decided to join in with him.

One of the guys from Texas threw down his cards, jumped up, and invited me to discuss the situation outside. I had done some boxing with him before so I figured I could take him without much trouble. I looked him in the eye and told him to forget about outside, he could have me right here. He stared at me a second or two and then sat back down.

My friend and I resumed our singing. We were sitting on our bunks with our backs to the card players. Halfway into the next song one of them threw a cup of water on the back of my head. I assumed it was the Texas fellow but because I hadn't seen him do it, I challenged the whole poker-playing lot of them to settle this outside. No one moved so I gave the Texan my best "I'll nail your carcass to the wall" look and sat down.

My buddy and I went back to singing, but the fun was gone. In a little bit I realized they were more in the right than I was. I told my buddy we should stop the singing. If nothing else, I had taught the Texan what it was to fear a country boy from Arkansas. It wasn't until later I found out he didn't throw the water. It was one of my fellow Arkansans.

More trouble broke out a few weeks later early on Christmas morning. I had forgotten we could sleep late that day. The guys were all taking advantage of the late reveille. I woke up in a panic, forgetting we had the day off. Knowing drill instructors did not approve of recruits sleeping late, I jumped out of my bunk, yelling and shaking everyone to get them up before the DI busted us. My kindness and thoughtfulness was' rewarded with a volley of cursing, thrown boots, and a few choice nicknames. Dumbass was one of the more polite ones. When the dust settled, I tried to apologize but that was like fuel on the fire. One recruit threatened to teach me a lesson and moved in on me. We tangled for a moment, then I grabbed him with a neck lock and gradually lowered him to the floor. Luckily, he was about my size, so the struggle ended well for me.

When we got back to the marine base one of the fellows asked me why I changed huts. I told him their bunch was just too tough for me. That seemed to please him.

All through boot camp I tried to be as inconspicuous as possible. I was not always successful. One day while standing at attention with our platoon, my mind wandered a bit. I did not realize that I was swaying slightly. Reality crashed in on me in the form of the drill instructor. He grabbed me by the neck of my sweatshirt and bellowed for me to stand straight and stop swaying. He turned me loose, picked up a rock, threw it wildly across the road, and muttered something about none of us were fit to be called marines. I remember hoping he shot better than he threw. But I was smart enough to keep that to myself.

The last week in boot camp we finally got it all together. We did not miss a step as the drill instructor marched us over to the graduation site. On our first day in training, he had told us we were about the worst bunch of recruits he had ever seen. After graduation, as we were waiting to be dispersed to go our separate ways, he wished us luck and congratulated us. He told us that we had come a long way and that we were about the finest platoon he had ever instructed.

I was assigned to signal training school as a telephone man. It would be four weeks before another class would start. Until then, most of the class's training was to march back and forth to the mess hall, do some calisthenics, and wash our clothes. Then we endured the really tough stuff—going on liberty and to the movies. This was the best duty I ever had in the marines. The food was excellent. Unlike my earlier training, the food included a wider selection of meats, vegetables, and even extra jellies. We did not have to go through a chow line. We were served by men who had just finished boot camp. We ate more like the officers did. I now was up to one hundred and fifty pounds. It looked like I would make a marine, after all.

Finally, we started the six-week training school for telephone men. This training consisted of electronic theory in the classroom. We then had more hands-on work like climbing telephone poles and making cable splices while up the pole. The poles had been climbed so much that any slipping with the hooks buckled to our legs meant splinters in our legs and stomach. Some of the fellows burned the poles from top to bottom. The class made it through without any serious injuries.

For the last week of training we went up in the mountains out from San Diego where an old CCC camp had been. There we simulated laying telephone wire for a full marine division and connecting up the switchboards. The first two days were very beautiful with clear sunshiny skies. The air was so fresh. The next day there was a six-inch snow that covered everything.

Early in training, my three-man crew outperformed the others. We did so well we were broken up and placed as leaders of our own three-man crews. My glory was short lived. Near the end of our training we had to lay wire and hook up switchboards like the kind used in combat. I had one of the most distant switchboards way out from anyone else. The instructor did not think my wire cabling was neat enough, so he put another man in charge of redoing the cabling. This may have cost me making corporal. Out of forty men only two made corporal. On the other hand, if I had made corporal, I would have most likely been placed in a battalion wire team, which would not have been my first choice.

After completing the six-week signal course, most of us were sent up to Camp Pendleton. There we received further training on laying telephone wire and hooking up switchboards for a whole marine division.

Training also included several practice beach landings. I got seasick, which was aggravated by the fumes from the diesel engine powering the craft. The landing craft would circle around waiting to head toward the beach, simulating a regular battle landing. This gave me more time to get seasick. One time I made it almost to the beach before having to heave over the side of the craft. Even at that it was a lot of fun sleeping out in the California night air in our pup tents with dew accumulating some on the grass by morning and eating the old type C-rations for the first time. I carried reels of telephone wire until I almost dropped.

After three days on our last big practice of landing and laying telephone wire, we marched back to our barracks. We were one stinking bunch of marines. After we shaved and showered, some of us went on liberty. That was the best I ever felt in my life. I was now up to one hundred and sixty-two pounds—one well-conditioned marine. One of my buddies told me my parents would be proud of me. It would be two years later before I would see them.

After training I was assigned to a real outfit called the Fourth Joint Assault Signal Company. This unit consisted of about four hundred marines and officers and a few sailors. Our main job would be to provide communications for the beachmaster and marine battalions to coordinate getting the proper supplies into the division. The supplies included everything from ammunition to food.

For each of the nine battalions there would be a naval gunfire spotting team and an air liaison team to provide bombing and strafing support. At first I was assigned to a beach party, but one day while at the Oceanside, California, marine base I was on a cleaning detail when a corporal from personnel came up. He asked me if there was a telephone man around who would volunteer to go to the Coronado Naval Base at San Diego to join a naval gunfire spotting team. I immediately volunteered.

Within thirty minutes I was on my way with my seabag to the Coronado Naval Base to hook up with the gunfire team that was short one telephone man. In this team were Lieutenant Monk Myers, the spotter; John Gann, the scout; John Klein and John Hein, radiomen; T. Rommel, a telephone man; and me, the new telephone man. I heard later my former sergeant back at Oceanside blew his stack and chewed out the corporal for not checking with him before taking one of his men without his permission. Sometimes in life, things can change a person's surroundings for better or worse. I thought this would be one exciting and lucky break for me. I was right.

Our training consisted of learning how to call up fire support and simulate directing fire by using the little hand-held walkie-talkie radio transmitters. One time I was embarrassed with all the fellows listening as I tried to simulate the calls over the hand-held. I was to say something like "up fifty yards, left thirty yards," as if correcting the gunfire. I lost my train of thought and didn't say anything. The instructor told me over the radio to come back inside. I was expecting a royal butt-chewing but instead all he said was, "It wasn't so easy, after all, now was it?"

In combat the spotter was to call the directions to our radio operator by telephone. Then the radio operator would transmit the directions to the ship, usually a destroyer, but at times a cruiser or a battleship. We practiced setting up the field radio transmitter, which was powered by a battery for the receiver. The transmitter was mounted on a little stand. The generator had a seat for a man to sit on while he cranked the generator using both hands. The radio gear was carried broken down in bags and had to be set up in the field by connecting the cables from the generator to the transmitter. The antenna was carried in a bag in sections that had to be screwed together and mounted on top of the transmitter.

To lighten our load we carried the smaller carbine for weapons. The scout had a Thompson submachine gun in case more firepower was needed. We practiced beach landings using small landing craft. After landing, we would set the radio up as we would in combat with the lieutenant calling the fire directions. Though our training was simulated, the lieutenant had actual gunfire-spotting training, having directed destroyer fire off a nearby island.

After one month we had the spotting down pat and could set the radio up in about five minutes. The idea was to have the spotter, the scout, and the one telephone man with his small reel of wire move out to a good observation site. One radio operator would receive the fire directions over the telephone and then relay the directions to the other radio operator. Most of the time the radio operator held the phone in one hand and the mike with the other hand while he talked to the ship. The telephone man cranked away on the generator while sweating profusely. The generator was not easy to crank, especially in over one-hundred-degree temperature. We later found out it would be even worse in the South Pacific heat.

Rommel, the first telephone man, wanted to be with the spotter. Since he was part of the original crew and I was the newcomer, he got his pick. That was fine with me. It was more dangerous to be with the spotter because he was near or at the front line most of the time. The radio transmitter was usually located near the battalion command post. That wasn't much different from anywhere else on the first day of attack during the early stages of a beach assault.

When we finished the naval gunfire training, we came back to Oceanside, where the rest of our outfit was located. We now were getting word we would be going overseas. We knew it would be in the Pacific, but where we were not told. The enemy had big ears and wanted to know our troop movements.

On June 6, 1944, I was on liberty in San Diego at a USO. That evening a man from a Christian group approached me and asked if I would like to pray with them for the soldiers at Normandy. Being a Christian, I naturally said yes. Some prayed in silence and several prayed aloud for the soldiers in Europe. We did not know that by September 15, 1944, in just a little over two months, our outfit would be in a similar situation at Peleliu, in the Pacific, five hundred miles from the Philippine Islands.

On June 29, we assembled at San Diego to embark for parts unknown in the Pacific. I was not too happy when I first saw the old Dutch ship, the *Polar Laute,* tied up at the dock. It was a dull gray ship that would take us away for a long time, which made me kind of sad. Some would not return alive.

All our trucks, jeeps, and gear were being loaded and tied down in the ship holds to be secure in case of heavy seas.

Our mail was censored and we could not tell our folks or friends that we were headed overseas. Though it was against orders, I'm sure some phone calls were made. I know for a fact I tried to call home. My parents did not have a phone, but I called some neighbors, hoping they would go get my parents, who lived only a fourth of a mile away. They had no boys in the service, only one daughter at home. Maybe they didn't understand the importance of that phone call, but no one went to get my parents. Those same neighbors came by our house one evening to welcome me home after the war. I was tempted to thank them for their "trouble" but let it go.

The old Dutch ship, built in 1929, had a wooden deck and one 3-inch gun mounted on the bow in case we were attacked. That did not seem like much protection to me.

We boarded the ship with over four hundred men and officers and with an extra eighteen hundred soldier replacements who were to get off at Honolulu, Hawaii. There was only one chow line for over twenty-two hundred men, and it would take almost four hours to feed that many men. I would get in line, then I would get seasick and go heave over the side and then get back in line. When I got to the galley on the lower deck the odor of sweating men mingled with the food smell sent me back up to top side again.

After that, my buddies in my gunfire team would bring me sandwiches while I lay in my bunk. John Hein and John Klein kept me going until we reached Honolulu some four days later. I will always be thankful for their gesture of good will. As long as I was lying down, I was okay. One of the fellows had his doubts that I would make it to Hawaii.

We stayed only three days in Honolulu. I tried to get word to my parents where I was by writing them that I had fresh pineapple for lunch. I found out later the letter had been censored and the word *pineapple* had been blacked out.

The captain lost no time in getting underway when it was time to leave. We did not know that a division of marines needed us soon to participate in their next campaign. I volunteered for shipboard guard duty so I would not have to wait in chow line. The seas were somewhat smooth as we sailed along without an escort, zigzaging all the way at a slow eleven knots an hour. It was peaceful at night as I stood watch looking out over the ocean as the ship cut through slightly rolling waves. During the day most of the men would play cards, both below and above deck, to pass the time away.

We celebrated the crossing of the equator. Those who were crossing for the first time received a certificate after being initiated as "shellbacks." Someone had brought out a ship fire hose and sprayed saltwater on some of the men as a symbol of being initiated. The saltwater shower was not unusual since rarely did we get to shower in fresh water. Most of the time we showered in sea water using a special soap. The voyage was peaceful and uneventful.

The ship's anchor was dropped off Quadalcanal on August 7, 1944, two years after the landing there by the First Marine Division on that date in 1942. Back then I was keeping up with the war over a battery-powered radio and the newspaper. Now I was with another bunch of kids who would help carry on the tradition of the First Marines.

One of our sergeants had made the original landing on Quadalcanal. I remember him saying this as we looked over the rail toward that island. We picked up a naval officer who would direct the old Dutch ship's captain into the Russell Islands about fifty miles away to Pavuvu, one of the islands in the Russell group. These islands were owned by the Dutch, who raised coconuts there.

As we sailed in among the Russell Islands I thought the jungle was beautiful. The trees and foliage came right up to the beach. They were greener than any woods or swamp in east Arkansas, but I realized the interiors of these islands might not be as nice as they looked.

Our ship eased in to a harbor at Pavuvu. There was a steel dock floating low on the water with a few marines looking out toward us, maybe thinking and wondering what the ship was going to do. The captain apparently was going to try to dock the ship without a tugboat. The ship seemed to be lined up fairly well with the dock, but we came in a little faster than we should have.

I watched from the deck as the dock got closer and closer without the ship slowing down. Just before we struck the dock, marines began running and diving off the dock into the water. It was comical to watch, but I hoped no one got hurt.

The dock was torn away from its mooring. The captain then began to steer the ship slowly out into the bay and dropped anchor. The dock was too badly damaged to use. The ship had to be unloaded by landing craft. As we climbed down nets we were taken off by smaller landing craft. It was a slow process.

Our group was sent over to the Third Battalion, First Marine Regiment of the First Marine Division. The First Marines had a rich history, being commanded by the famous Colonel Chesty Puller. Several tents had been set up for our thirty men not far from the mess hall. The streets were laid out neatly with coral used for the pavement. They reminded me of the gravel roads back home. The tents were arranged neatly in rows. In the tents the cots all had mosquito netting for protection. All in all, everything appeared to be clean.

Looking up at the tall palm trees, I could see large coconuts covered with green husks. There were fallen coconuts scattered on the ground. New arrivals would sometimes attack the coconuts with their machetes to remove the husk to get to the hard shell of the coconuts. Once in a while a coconut would fall from a great height, but I never heard of anyone getting hurt.

Pavuvu was not a good place to train marines. There was no place to maneuver. The first group of marines to arrive had a hard time of building streets, clearing away the rotting coconuts, and making the place livable. By the time we arrived, things were looking a little better. As an attached unit, we did not have the strict military nonsense to put up with, although we did have rifle inspection by one of the battalion officers.

There were over fifteen thousand men on the island, six men to a tent. That made for a lot of tents. The officers had separate tent areas and didn't eat with the enlisted men. They had extra issues of wine and alcohol, whereas the enlisted men had only beer, when it was available. That would be about every two weeks at a cost of ten cents a bottle. All the beer came in bottles since the aluminum can was not yet in use.

Since I did not drink beer, I traded mine for cokes. There was no ice so I drank most of my cokes in the cool of the morning. When there were no cokes I sold my beer for the same price I paid. One guy would sell his beer issue for seventy-five cents a bottle. That was a high price in those days, but he had no trouble selling it. I just would not do that to my buddies.

In about a week we had our first beer issue along with some cokes. Our lieutenant, Monk Myers, let Hein have two bottles of his wine and whiskey issue to pass around to us enlisted men. Since I didn't drink beer, they tried to get me to drink the wine or the whiskey. I finally gave in to Hein's encouragement and went for it. The liquor went down satisfactorily. The others kept drinking beer while I kept experimenting with the stronger stuff.

I got a little tipsy and not having learned my lesson during the basic training poker songfest, I opened up with a rendition of "Red River Valley." We had two hand-held walkie-talkies. Hein handed me one and took the other one down to our latrine. Several fellows were there relieving themselves of all the beer they had been drinking. Hein convinced them that the small hand-held radio, which would transmit less than a mile, was picking up a country music station from the United States.

One fellow said, "That can't be Roy Acuff."

Hein said, "It sure sounds like Roy Acuff."

Another fellow from the South said, "That sure makes me homesick."

Hein came back to the tent just as I was running out of songs.

I don't know if the guys in the latrine ever figured out why the radio station was playing the same singer over and over.

It was nearing dusk by this time and the fellows wanted to go to the outdoor movies, which had logs hewed flat on one side for seats. Each fellow had about a three-quarter case of beer left stowed safely under his cot. Someone had to guard the beer, so somebody suggested I watch it since I was in no shape to go to the movies. I was agreeable so they left their beer under my watchful eye.

After they left I got sick and heaved over the side of the cot just outside the tent flap. After heaving I got sleepy and groggy. I can vaguely remember a marine entering the tent and asking if I had any beer to sell. I said no. He left, but realizing that I was pretty groggy, told his friends they could sneak back to my tent and steal the beer.

The next thing I knew my buddies came in from the movies. They started looking for their beer, but it was gone. They began hollering and cursing. I was accused of selling it, giving it away, and even losing it. I sat up and shamefully and sorrowfully apologized and promised to give them all my beer when we got our next issue. That wasn't good enough for some of them, but several of the others realized it wasn't my fault. After all, they were the ones who got me drunk in the first place.

That was the first and only time I ever got drunk. Being from a Baptist family, I never told my parents about it.

The four weeks we were at Pavuvu was a busy time. We practiced our radio setups, perfected digging foxholes, and attended orientation meetings with officers explaining the battle plans. They showed us enlarged photo maps of Peleliu and explained how we would secure the airfield in three days. This did happen, but to completely wipe out the twelve thousand Japanese, it took two and a half months. We even had to use the army's Eighty-first Division, which was our backup reserve.

Even with all the activity, we still had some spare time. One afternoon our complete group was together. This included air liaison, naval gunfire, and the beach communication party for a total of about thirty men. We had some boxing gloves and were doing what you might call friendly sparing.

The original planners thought that a few navy personnel would make our group coordinate better with the ships. Although they were swell guys, I believe they needed more marine training for our activities. Appenzeller, a good friend of mine from Minnesota, was one of the navy men attached to our group. He was about six feet, two inches and weighed about two hundred pounds. He had boxed some in the past and had shown me some boxing techniques. This helped me because I had sparred a lot but hadn't much in the way of technical skills. At that time I was in good shape and weighed a hundred sixty-two pounds.

After messing around most of the afternoon sparring some with a fellow marine named Elliphenson, another marine named Soto from the air liaison group came up. He had just gotten off mess duty. Soto was part Hispanic, stood about five feet, eleven inches, and weighed one hundred eighty-five pounds. He was also an experienced boxer.

Soto wanted in on the action, but no one wanted to take him on. Most knew of his speed and boxing ability. Since no one wanted to box him, I volunteered. I thought a little sparring would not hurt much because that was all we had been doing. As soon as I made the offer, one of the air liaison fellows decided to make it more like a real boxing match. He "recommended" two rounds, three minutes each.

I did not like this at all and was pretty shook up. I thought the guy was doing a lot of recommending for someone who wasn't stepping into the ring. My confidence took another hit when Elliphenson told me he thought Soto would kill me. Having made an offer to box, though, I didn't want to back out in front of everyone.

Soto wasn't the best liked fellow, but was not a bad guy. I noticed he, too, seemed to have a little reservation. After getting the gloves on, the timing guy said go. I thought I would feel Soto out by throwing a straight right jab to the chin. The blow caught him by surprise. He moved, stumbled backward, and fell flat on his back. The blow did not actually knock him down, but it looked that way to the other fellows. I thought to myself that I wished I had not done that.

Soto was embarrassed. He got up and came at me, moving and feinting as good boxers do, with both gloves hammering the air. He got in close and began to tap me with fast jabs. The only way I would survive would be to keep him off me. I resorted to the old country boy's method of throwing round-house rights. Not many even connected.

Soto would move in and land lightning-fast hits, though not hard ones. I handled these fairly well. The first round was over. There was one more to go.

In the second round I began using some of Appenzeller's pointers, a quick left to the stomach followed by a quick right to the head. Soto was quick. I got the blow to the stomach but missed with the right as he ducked under the blow. We kept up a pretty good pace until the round was over—which was enough for a hot day.

Soto had landed three blows to my one, although I hit harder. I was surprised when the air liaison fellow called it a draw. That night at the movies I could still feel the effects of Soto's punches, but did not let on. Elliphenson advised me to try out for the division boxing exhibition. Our gunfire team was rather proud of the way I represented the team, out-weighed by twenty pounds. Soto and I never boxed again. I don't believe either one of us wanted to take the other on again.

The Fourth JASCO was organized to give better communication for naval gunfire, air liaison, and beach support for the beachmaster to get needed supplies to the troops. The naval gunfire team and the air liaison team were to go in with the third wave. All nine battalions had identical teams like ours, which was the Third Battalion, First Regiment, of the First Marine Division.

Facing the beach would be our Third Battalion on the extreme left, which, as it turned out, would catch the hottest resistance early on. Next was the First Battalion, followed by the Second Battalion, and three battalions of the Fifth Regiment. The Seventh Regiment lined up on the far right with their Second Battalion in reserve.

The First Division had only 10,000 true infantry to face 12,000 well-dug-in Japanese. The Japanese were also protected by extensive pillboxes and caves, some up to five stories deep in the coral hills. Some 6,000 of the Japanese troops were elite soldiers from out of Manchuria.

This matchup was not the ideal military strategy. An assault like the one we planned should have a three to one ratio for assault against defense. The balance of the First's force was about 10,000 more men in the support troops with tanks, artillery, supply, headquarters, and other auxiliaries such as the Fourth JASCO. One-third of our marines were veterans, another third had limited experience, but the remaining third now faced their first battle. They were kids just out of high school, eighteen to twenty years old.

The main purpose of the assault was to deny the Japanese the use of the airfield and protect General MacArthur's flank before he was to hit the Philippines one month later.

As we began to load up for Peleliu, my thoughts were on Bob Hope and a show he did for the First Marine Division at our base on Pavuvu. His group was flown into Pavuvu by two of the Piper Club mail planes. They landed on the main roadway that served as our airstrip. I remember Bob Hope, Jerry Colonna, Patti Thomas, and Frances Lankford all waved as their little planes landed. I was right beside the roadway and had a good view.

Bob told his usual number of jokes. Jerry was the straight man. Patti danced in a bathing suit, and Frances sang. There was much cheering and applause with the whole division enjoying the show. Years later Bob told about the show in *Reader's Digest,* saying he was sad knowing that some marines would never make it home. That day, being the showman he was, you would never have known it. After the show was over I walked back to my tent area. One of the fellows noticed I looked sad and asked me what was wrong . I told him the show had made me think of home and I was getting lonely. Maybe it was a premonition of things to come, but I did not tell him that.

While preparing for the trip to Peleliu, we put our radio gear in waterproof bags about the size of a small trunk. I reminded Hein not to forget the extra battery for the radio receiver. Hein told me just to take care of my business, the telephone equipment, and he'd handle the radio equipment just fine. I said OK and dropped it. As it turned out, on the third day after landing at Peleliu the battery played out. It took about three hours to go back to the supply headquarters to get a battery, but they didn't have the one we needed. They had to let us have a different spare radio transmitter. I never said anything like "I told you so" to Hein. It would not have helped matters any.

Colonel Chesty Puller was in charge of the First Regiment, which we were with during the loading of the equipment. I remember quite well watching him at the loading zone walking around looking over the situation. He was a short stocky marine with a big chest. I could see why he was called "Chesty."

Our LST (U.S. Navy Landing Ship-Tank) was being loaded with amphibious tractors. There was one frail duck the air liaison team would use. The duck did not have the protection like the tractors. Everything went rather well getting our gear on to the LST, except our equipment and all of our team would have to stay topside on the deck during the trip up to Peleliu. By later

Bloodynose Ridge, Peleliu (Palau Group), September 12–14, 1944, bombardment of heavily fortified positions of Japanese. *USMC photo, courtesy Nimitz Museum.*

accounts, not enough LSTs were available, so the troops were stuffed in the best way possible. A number of troopships had to be used, which put a burden getting the marines into action by transferring to landing craft at the battle site. At the time I did not know any different and assumed it was planned that way. Only a few men were left behind that were in the motor pool. Hardly any of our jeeps and trucks were loaded due to the fact that these were really not needed, at least not by us.

In early September, the ships were loaded and ready for the voyage up to Peleliu. We were to make our assault on September 15, 1944. The voyage was uneventful, except for the one night it rained. Some of us slept under a large tarp, but someone had left the rubber bag open that contained our radio transmitter and there was a fold in the tarp, letting water drain down into the open bag, covering the chassis of the transmitter. Lieutenant Myers was extremely unhappy. Hein took the transmitter out and dried it in the hot sun. We were not allowed to fire up the transmitter but did turn on the battery power. The tubes seemed to light properly. The question now was whether or not the radio transmitter would work when we landed. Our backup transmitter was on another LST with Klein, our other radio operator, with a reserve team of marines under a navy officer in case our team got knocked out. Actually, in the landing it was their radio transmitter that got knocked out.

Being fresh and young, I felt somewhat optimistic about our chances of success, but Rommel and Gann, in their mid-twenties and early thirties, thought some of us might not make it through the campaign.

We were now almost at Peleliu. Everything was in order for the assault. There were a great number of ships about, and the navy had begun the bombardment of Peleliu to soften it up for the First Marine Division and the Eighty-first Army Division. The Eighty-first was to hit Anguar, a much smaller island next to Peleliu with about nine hundred Japanese defenders.

On September 14, we were told to recheck our gear. We were to have two canteens filled with water, a belt with extra carbine rounds, a backpack with eating utensils, toilet articles like toothbrush, soap, and razor, a change of underwear, and other odds and ends. We had a shovel attached to our backpacks. Our weapon would be the carbine, for close-range firing. We also were issued a gas mask, which, thankfully, never had to be used. In addition to all that we had an inflatable belt life preserver strapped around our waist. That was one thing we could drop after the landing.

We were told to hit the sack early, get up by 0500, eat breakfast, and be ready to climb down into the amphibious tractor with all our packs and communication gear when the word was given. It was a heck of a load.

I slept better than I expected, but the 0500 hour came all too soon. My appetite was not too good. The tension was building. After breakfast we got all our gear on and readied the communication equipment.

We were told by our officer we would be going in with the battalion commander and his staff. Since our team was small, it would mean only about twelve men and the two drivers for the amphibious tractor. With all our gear it would be a snug fit.

Around 0700 we climbed down the ladder to the tractor deck and got in the tractor. Some newer tractors had the rear ramp that could be lowered and raised. Ours did not. We had to climb over the sides and down into the compartment hole.

Lieutenant Colonel Stephen V. Sabol, the battalion commander, positioned his staff in the front of the tractor's small cargo space with our team in the rear. Appenzeller, the sailor attached to our team, was in the very rear. As I looked across the lower deck I saw the big blond-headed kid with air liaison climbing across the front of the duck that would carry them in. It was the last time I was ever to see him alive. Their duck was blown up and their radio gear lost. To my knowledge our air liaison team never got into operation the first day. It was left up to naval gunfire to give the main support. Except for Soto, I never saw any of the air liaison until we got back to Pavuvu.

The tractor drivers began cranking their machines. I then realized we were committed. Whatever was going to happen to us would happen. Our fate would be battling our faith from this point on.

There was the usual military "hurry up and wait" procedure. The timing had to be right for this massive orchestration of men and equipment to give success a better chance. We were all afraid, but our marine training would carry us through. We had made many practice landings but never one out of an LST.

The skies are blackened with smoke from the combined naval and aerial bombardment of the Peleliu beach, as landing craft scurry shoreward with the marine assault troops who gained a toehold on that Japanese bastion flanking the southeastern Philippines. *USMC photo.*

Naval craft bombard the Peleliu beach as a softener for the marine assault troops who hit the beach in the initial landing. *USMC photo.*

As supporting naval and air units pave the way with high-velocity explosives, marine-laden assault craft form the first wave and move in for the attack on Peleliu. *USMC photo.*

Marines wounded in the initial landings at Peleliu are huddled under a duck (amphibious truck), which will take them to one of the transports. *USMC photo.*

Thank God for the people who built this huge armada of ships that would carry us to victory. This time I was not part of a rag-tag football team, but a highly trained and well-equipped marine force that was prepared to give it their all. The Marine Corps had pounded into us that we could not fail. I felt confident that we would accomplish our mission.

The big doors on the bow swung open. My stomach took a nasty turn. This was more serious than a kickoff at a high school football game. The tractor engines revved up. Even with the doors fully open the engine exhaust choked me and aggravated my already sick stomach. I was ready for some fresh air.

The front machine lurched forward. In a moment our tractor was scraping away on the steel deck. The machine rolled down the ramp and settled into the sea. The tracks began churning the ocean water. I scanned the scene from north to south as my attention was caught by the big battleships bellowing fire and smoke as they hurled big shells toward the shore. The sound was worse than the heaviest thunderstorm I ever remembered.

The shoreline was covered with black smoke mixed with the fires of hades as the shells exploded. Some of the shells kicked up sand and ocean spray as they fell short of their target. To my right were hundreds of amphibious tractors circling around waiting for the signal to line up for the run to the beach.

I didn't have to wait long before the navy patrol crafts had the tractors lined up. Sailors on nearby ships were giving us the V for victory sign. Seeing their good wishes gave some encouragement.

We needed the tractors to get past the seven hundred yards of coral reef that the landing craft could not cross. The later waves in the landing craft had to wait for the tractors to return and pick them up. The marines in the sixth wave really caught it worse than we did because by then the smoke had lifted some and the Japanese could see their target better. At the time I was not aware of this situation, but was occupied by our immediate circumstances.

The aircraft took over as the naval gunfire lifted. Wave after wave of navy and marine dive bombers strafed the beach area, dropping bombs inland a little ways off the beach.

The signal was given. The long lineup of the first three waves headed for the beach about three minutes apart. My tension let up a little as we seemed to meet no opposition. This quickly changed.

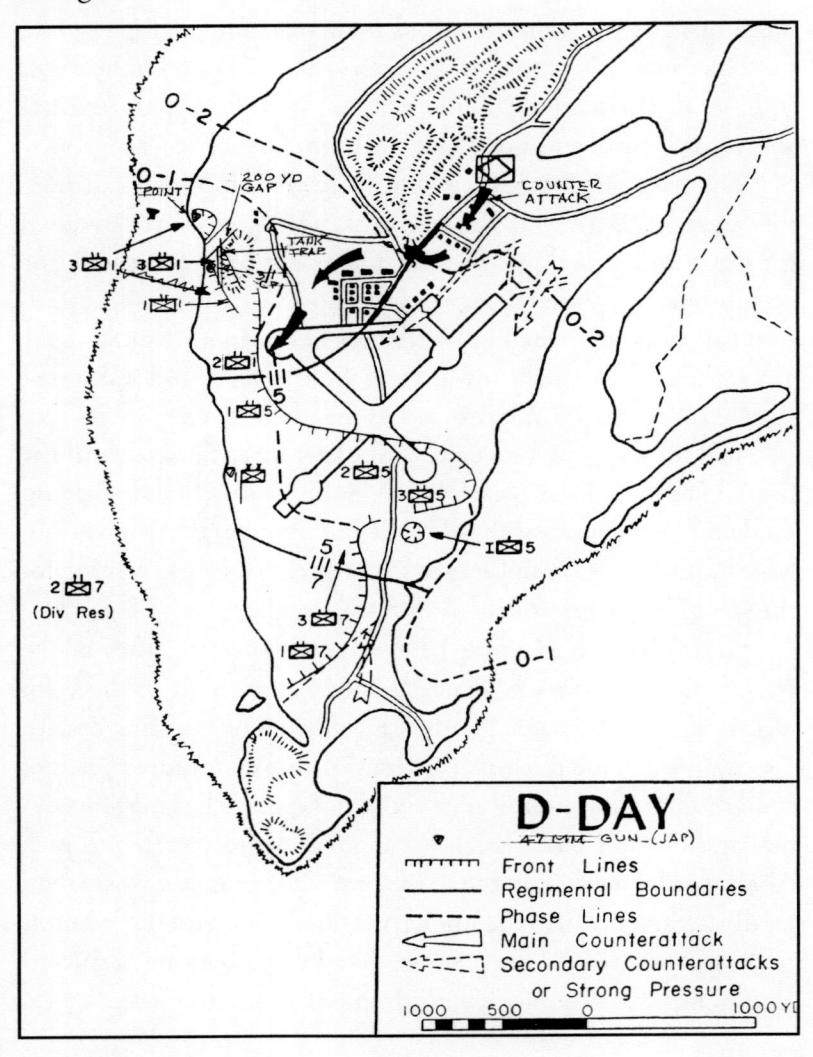

30 THUNDER IN THE MORNING

More marines wounded in the initial landings at Peleliu are huddled in a duck as they wait to be taken to transports lying offshore. *USMC photo.*

Marines of the First Division, pinned down by heavy mortar fire, remain near their equipment as they hit "Orange Beach 3" on Peleliu. Amtracs, hit while carrying the green-clad leathernecks ashore, burn in the background. *USMC photo.*

Off to our right two tractors exploded in fire, followed by smaller explosions around us coming from Japanese mortar rounds. One of the officers yelled for everybody to get down low. I glanced back toward Appenzeller and saw him turn pale. Being taller than most of us, he could see over the side better. He later said three mortar shells followed us in. I did see what I thought was a splash once as I raised my head out of curiosity, but I quickly ducked back down as the treads began scraping the top of the coral reef.

By this time the Japanese had really opened up with their 47 mm gun from the point. They were raising havoc as our tractor scraped hard against the coral. We pitched like a bucking bronco, crashing over holes in the coral as we closed in on the shore. The tractor tilted its nose up as we began to crawl up the beach. The driver drove the tractor about twenty yards and stopped.

The two drivers got on the two front-mounted machine guns and began spraying fire over the heads of the first two waves toward a small hill ridge line. The tractor front end was tilted up slightly. Everyone climbed out over the side and jumped to the sandy beach. Hein had the main radio transmitter, and since it was heavy, another marine helped him with it. I handed the generator and the other equipment out as fast as I could. I made sure there was nothing left. As I handed the last item out, the antenna bag, the driver put the tractor in reverse. He yelled at me to hurry up because he had to get back and pick up more marines. The tractor was already backing up as I climbed over the side.

The residue from the shells stung my nostrils. There was a slight haze from the smoke. I then heard the most awful noise of my life. Machine-gun and rifle fire mixed with mortar fire ripped through the air.

Monk was just ahead of me. He was wearing glasses. He looked strange wearing those glasses because I had never seen him wear any before now. That added to the unreality of the

Wrecks of amphibious landing craft smoulder on the Peleliu beach after they were put out of action by Japanese gunfire. *USMC photo.*

Lieutenant Colonel R. G. Ballance, Champagne, Illinois, of the First Marine Division, resumes his duties as commander of the Pioneer Battalion, despite shrapnel wounds received on the Peleliu beach. *USMC photo.*

moment—all hell breaking out around me and there was Lieutenant Myers wearing new glasses.

Monk motioned us forward, crouching to avoid the bullets passing over him. The rest of us imitated him as we moved farther inland off the beach.

Pure fear gripped me. I had read about battle casualties before entering the service. Now I knew fellow marines were being torn apart by enemy fire. This was no newspaper article *about* war. This was me *in* war. This was about my *life*.

At this point, all our training and practice paid off. We automatically went into our training exercise mode. We crept forward about fifty yards. Monk called us to a halt behind a fallen palm tree lying parallel with the beach. There was not a tree standing, just stumps where trees had been. At this spot, thankfully, there was no coral, just sand. Monk ordered Hein to set up the radio. Hein began mounting the radio on the short legs as I got the generator mounted on a small support, which had a seat and two handles for cranking the generator. Next I connected the flexible cable from the generator to the transmitter, while Hein screwed the antenna sections to the insulator mounted on top of the radio transmitter. Hein turned on the battery power for the radio receiver and began tweaking the knobs. He told me to give him some generator power so he could get the destroyer's radio zeroed to ours. The dried-out transmitter fired without missing a beat. It worked! Thank God! In no time Hein had the destroyer on our receiver asking for directions.

Monk then ordered Gann and Rommel to follow him so they could get targets for the destroyer. They headed north parallel with the beach up toward the point where some of George Hunt's Company K of the Third Battalion was supposed to be. Rommel was stringing the small reel of telephone wire as he followed Monk and Gann.

Everything was working just like a training exercise. I had

begun to control my fear and started digging a fairly large foxhole near the transmitter. I read in later years that when men go into battle and are given something to do, they are much calmer. I believe it.

The noise of battle had not slacked off, but had actually gotten worse. Waiting to hear from Monk, I told myself not to look back toward the ships, but to keep focused on what we had to do. It would not have helped for me to see the sixth wave being battered badly. I couldn't help them anyway.

I had wondered why Monk didn't take us farther inland. He had made the right decision. Not too far from where we were, Company K's second platoon was being wiped out in a fifteen-foot-wide tank trap. They were being pulverized by heavy machine-gun and rifle fire from entrenched and heavily fortified Japanese troops on a twenty-five-foot-high ridge just behind the tank trap. Over two-thirds of Company K's Second platoon were killed or wounded. The survivors were penned down until late that afternoon. Up at the point, the balance of Company K was getting hit hard.

Things were happening fast. Hein and I had dug our two foxholes quickly in the loose sand while waiting to hear from Monk. At last Monk came in over the phone saying he had a target for the destroyer. Hein called in the target coordinates given by Monk and the destroyer sent in a shell.

Monk began to direct the fire. When the naval gunfire was on target, Monk would call for five guns to fire ten salvos. I could hear the shells exploding like thunder, drowning out even the noise of the machine-gun and rifle fire. The destroyer fired fifty rounds a minute. If there were any Japanese in there, they never knew what hit them.

Monk kept calling in different coordinates, moving the shelling into different areas in front of our lines. Rommel crawled back to us and informed us the 47 mm Japanese gun at the point had been knocked out by K Company, which made us all feel better. Rommel did not stay long, but soon headed back up to where Monk and Gann were.

After roughing up the sixth wave out on the reef, the Japanese began to work the beach over some more. They dropped mortars, starting at the point where Company K was and then worked south along a line that was just about in the middle of the beach. Most of our service troops were in this area.

The mortar rounds were evenly spaced along the entire length of the beach. We could hear the whine of each round before it hit and exploded. I felt helpless as the rounds struck closer and closer. I was still sweating it out when the mortars passed over me and landed farther down the beach.

On the first mortar attack, one of the rounds landed just north of me as Lieutenant Colonel Sabol, our battalion commander, jumped in beside me in my somewhat enlarged foxhole. I knew he was nearby but was surprised to see him jump into my foxhole.

The next round landed just south of us, followed by another round that sprayed one of our beach party marines with shrapnel. Someone hollered for a corpsman. The wounded marine was covered in blood. Two marines got him on a stretcher and headed toward the beach. I thought I would never see him alive again but when we got back to Pavuvu, he hardly had a scratch showing.

Watching the wounded man being carried to safety, Lieutenant Colonel Sabol muttered that he couldn't believe he was in a foxhole with a PFC. I didn't know whether to be flattered or insulted. I thought about looking him in the eye and saying that, heck, I'd had a full bird colonel in here just twenty minutes earlier. I refrained.

Sabol had wound up in my foxhole because his corporal guard had yelled for him to jump into what he thought was a mortar shell hole. Battlefield mythology held no two shells land in the same place. Thus, you were safe inside a freshly exploded shell hole.

When the corporal shouted for the lieutenant colonel to jump, he did not address him by rank for fear a Japanese soldier might be within hearing distance. Officers did not want to be called by rank in battle, for fear the enemy would go for them ahead of others. A few moments later, Sabol moved out of my foxhole and found another one nearby, I think with another officer.

The mortar attack rolled on down the beach toward the Fifth Regiment. After this attack the Japanese repeated the mortar shelling. This was now really getting to me. I don't know who knocked out the mortar, but the mortars finally stopped falling. Thankfully! It is possible that our naval gunfire got the mortar. Or one of K Company's marines, up near the point where the hottest action was, took it out. I probably could get some argument on that.

The action continued as Monk kept the destroyer busy with ten 5-gun salvos a minute. All at once we lost the telephone line. I got off the generator, picked up my carbine, and started following the telephone line. A short way from the radio were three marine riflemen. One had his big toe about shot off. I could see where the bullet had torn away the front of his shoe. I told him he needed to get that taken care of. He replied that it was not bothering him much. I'll never forget his attitude, that he would not let this distract him from his duty. One of the other marines warned me about a sniper in the brush. I asked him why he didn't go get him. He gave me a peculiar look. I realize now that the sniper had probably been firing from the ridge where so many Japanese were located.

I proceeded along the telephone line and saw bullets kicking up sand just in front of me. I raced across the spot and got behind a fallen coconut tree. After I caught my breath, I looked over the fallen tree. Right in front of me was Rommel, splicing the line break. He was standing up, making a good target, as if there were not a war going on. He let me know there were two more breaks in the line. I saw one break just across the log and went to work on it.

When Rommel finished splicing the break he was working on, he told me to get the last one. I told him he was closer to it than I was and for him to get it. I headed back to the radio. Rommel wasn't too happy about it.

When I got back to the radio, Rommel had finished the splice. Hein and Monk were in communication with each other. I thought we are really cooking. Then the telephone went dead again. The small light wire, which was laid parallel to the beach, was too exposed to traffic and the mortars.

The telephone line had become a serious problem. Monk sent Gann and Rommel back to our radio location until the line could be repaired. After Gann and Rommel located themselves just behind us toward the beach, Gann caught a bullet that tore almost through his right knee. That probably saved Rommel's life, because his head was positioned just past Gann's knee. Rommel called for a stretcher. Gann was groaning as he was carried toward the beach. I never saw him again.

Major Jonas M. Platt, third in command of the Third Battalion, came over to where Hein was and asked if he could be of help. Hein said we had lost our telephone line. Major Platt volunteered to call the fire, since he had all the know-how on the five-inchers from battleship duty. He got on the radio and talked with the destroyer's commander, explaining our situation. Major Platt, being an officer, had access to the battle maps. He immediately began feeding coordinates for the targets. He had the destroyer firing on his best guess since we did not have a hill from which to observe.

Major Platt called up the company commanders, using the

SCR300 radios, and asked them where they needed help the most. He then had the destroyer work the area over.

Being on the generator stand I could hear most of the conversations. At times the commanders at the battle site would describe some of the Japanese activities, like "I see the little bastard sneaking around trying to get set up to fire on us."

My battalion was on the extreme left of the battle front. The other battalions had not penetrated very deep and had not crossed the airfield. That being the case, the destroyer could lie off to our left and cover our entire front line. About noon our destroyer had used up all the shells they were allowed to fire. They were down to the reserve and had to go pick up more ammo. Major Platt told the destroyer's captain to get another destroyer in position as fast as he could.

Pretty soon the other destroyer came in on our frequency, saying they were in position and were waiting for fire directions. Major Platt wasted no time getting them a target. After they had the range, he had them let go with five-gun salvos. Once when a company officer said we were helping, Major Platt had the destroyer go into continuous five-gun salvos. After a while the destroyer's captain called on the radio and asked that his sailors get a rest because they were dead tired, exhausted. Major Platt thanked the captain for their fine effort and agreed. The destroyer's captain wanted to know what effect the shelling was having. Major Platt told the captain that if he got up out of his hole, he'd get his head "blowed off." As he got word from the companies, Major Platt later let the captain know that the fire from the Japanese had decreased considerably. The mortars had stopped sometime earlier.

Things had been going so good with Major Platt calling the fire in from the second destroyer that we kind of forgot about Monk up near the point with Company K. I heard a marine state that we should have already had someone checking on him and should have had the telephone line back in service. I heard someone say that since I was the telephone man, I should try and reach Monk. I agreed but said I wasn't going out unless I had a rifleman to watch out for snipers. No one wanted to go with me.

By then we were all done in by the high temperature and from cranking the generator. Appenzeller had been helping me crank on the generator so I asked him to go with me. He said that as a navy man, he wasn't trained for that sort of thing. I understood his feeling and did not consider him a coward.

Major Platt finally rounded up a marine rifleman, the last man left in his squad not killed or wounded. The rifleman agreed to go with me. Reluctantly, we took off following the telephone line, knowing Monk should be somewhere near the end of the telephone line. We had gone about one-third of the way when we heard the crack of rifle fire. We hit the deck and lay there as we tried to figure out from where the rifle fire was coming.

All at once a chunk of wood exploded right near my face. The sniper had zeroed in. Now it was decision time, to risk going on or be the coward. In my decision, I knew Major Platt was doing a good job, even better than Monk, because he had communication with the company commanders, whereas Monk didn't. I favored the better part of valor and told the rifleman to do what he wanted, I was going back.

I wasted no time getting back. I missed the radio site by going too much toward the beach. Recognizing that I had missed the radio site, I turned and came in a little to the right side. As I came up, one of the crew asked why I was coming in from that side. He then asked a question that stabbed me in the heart. He wanted to know if I even went out there. This made me mad. I gritted my teeth and told him he didn't even try to go. Major Platt seemed to understand and did not criticize me.

I always regretted down through the years not getting through to Monk and thought I was a coward for it. Some fifty years later I read an account of the Peleliu invasion in Hunt's *Coral Comes*

Saturation bombardment of Peleliu on September 15, 1944, was the heaviest bombardment by the U.S. Navy until this time. *USMC photo.*

Shown here is one of the twenty miniature Jap tanks that made the counterattack about 4:30 P.M., September 15, 1944. *USMC photo, courtesy Nimitz Museum.*

High. Hunt described the two-hundred-yard gap between the battalion command post (CP) and his company. Over a hundred Japanese had infiltrated into the gap. It took over thirty hours for B Company of the Seventh Regiment to remove them. They had been called in by Colonel Sabol with permission from division headquarters. I felt somewhat redeemed. Our telephone line was just inside that gap.

After the battle, on the way to Okinawa, Monk questioned me in front of our team about the incident. I told Monk I had made every reasonable effort to reach him, including the part about the sniper missing my face by inches. He never said anything more about it. He further vindicated me in a backhanded manner later on Okinawa when he criticized me for bringing batteries up to his lookout site at the front by myself. He told me not to do that again, adding if I got hit, he wanted someone with me.

By midafternoon the second destroyer had used up all the ammo it was allowed to fire and had left the scene. Major Platt was able to get a third destroyer to replace the second one. The action had slowed somewhat but Major Platt was still getting some fire in where he thought it would help. It was impossible to tell just how effective the destroyers were. I believe our gunfire helped because the enemy fire had almost stopped. The noise had abated and I was feeling a little more secure. That soon changed.

At 4:30 P.M., the battalion master sergeant yelled over to us that the Japanese were counterattacking and any minute would break through in tanks. I felt powerless. What good would my carbine be against the thick hide of a tank? Hein handed me a phosphorous smoke grenade, but I still had my doubts about the coming battle. I asked him what I could do with only one phosphorous smoke grenade. Maybe Hein thought I was brave enough to get on top of a tank and drop the grenade inside. All I know is that it felt good in my hand. Word finally came through that the attack had been stopped and the tanks had been destroyed. My, what a relief!

It was getting late into the afternoon and part of our backup radio crew had begun to show up. Captain Johnson, the navy officer in charge of the backup crew, said Klein had been shot through the wrist and a bullet had penetrated the radio transmitter on his back, making it useless. He added that Klein had been evacuated and would be all right. As dusk was approaching Monk finally showed up. He didn't get a scratch through the whole ordeal. I was especially relieved, as was the whole team.

The colonel had been looking for a volunteer to take a message up to K Company just as Monk appeared. I realized it was an opportunity to be a hero. Whoever carried the message through would most likely get a medal. The opportunity passed as I heard Monk say he knew where they were and would carry the message. The colonel handed Monk the message and thanked him for volunteering. A large amphibious tractor had just shown up with supplies for K Company and was available for Monk to ride. I enviously thought I would have volunteered if I had known about the tractor. Most likely, Monk did not know about the tractor when he volunteered. Before Monk left he thanked Major Platt for carrying on while he was up at the point.

As Hunt tells it in *Coral Comes High*, Monk Myers and Dolan had come over the cliff–after sneaking through a coconut grove. What he did not know was that Monk actually rode the tractor up and had walked over the rise where he and Dolan found Hunt.

Monk told Hunt he was isolated and surrounded by Japanese and asked if he thought he could hold. Hunt replied that he could, then muttered that it looked like "we'll have to." Monk then wished him luck and said he was going to swim back outside the reef to get back.

All the destroyers had been ordered to pull away from shore and get out into the open sea, except a couple left for shooting flares for the night. We kept waiting for Monk to return. It was nearly 10:00 P.M. when Monk showed up. He said he had been delayed trying to avoid some Japanese who were trying to sneak in on us.

Monk only had on his skivies. He had to remove his dungarees in order to swim back. He was cold and shivering. It could be cool at night even at that latitude in the South Pacific. No dungarees could be found for him. Major Platt was somehow able to find a pair of ragged khaki trousers and shirt. We decided we did not want our officer dressed in ragged khakis, so Hein suggested I give Monk my dungarees and wear the ragged khakis. He finished me off with "you're about Monk's size, anyway." The dungarees fit Monk just fine. I put on the ragged khakis but I was not very happy about it. Hein practically worshiped Monk.

The next day Monk said to me that my dungarees sure were dirty. I gritted my teeth and told him I had been *fighting a war*, which should explain the dirt, mud, and sweat. Monk wore the dungarees for at least five days. I wore the ragged khakis until I got back to Pavuvu. About the third day Major Platt said he needed to get me a better set of clothes. He left and I never saw him again.

To me, Major Platt was one of the unsung heros on Peleliu. He came in and did what needed to be done. It was a critical time and probably prevented the Japanese from organizing and attacking through the gap. That would have been disastrous for the Third Battalion and for the First Regiment.

Later that night I jolted awake. I didn't know what time it was because I did not carry a watch. All hell was breaking loose up at the point. The Japanese were trying to wipe out Hunt's small reduced marine force so they could push down the beach and attack our flank. The gap was not defended. One of the mysteries of the Japanese strategy is why they did not attack through the gap. I suppose they wanted to make sure their rear was protected before breaking through for their main push.

Hunt's little band of thirty-five marines just barely held their ground. The next morning over a hundred dead Japanese were found around the point. If they had broken through, our team would not have survived. Our headquarters group was not armed adequately to have stopped them. It wasn't until later that I learned the full implication behind Hunt's heroic struggle. They say ignorance is bliss. I agree.

The morning of the second day came. I felt somewhat rested and ate some field rations. I made a cup of hot chocolate in my tin cup, using a few small sticks. By the time we reached Okinawa many months later, I had gotten good at building a small fire.

Some changes were now in order. Hunt had gone through the night without any communication with the battalion CP. The next morning a telephone line was laid to Hunt's Company K along the reef, but the line was severed as soon as Hunt began to talk to Colonel Sabol. Someone failed to consider all the traffic a line running parallel to the beach had to take. And it didn't help being exposed to all the mortars and gunfire taking place.

Monk told battalion headquarters he had to have a set of SCR300 radios if he was going to do any good. That morning someone on the battalion staff got him a set of SCR300s and a radio operator. One of the SCR300s was set up near our larger radio transmitter, which was used for ship communication. Monk used the other SCR300 to relay information back to us.

Our telephone line was the only one laid to the point that first day. Even with the lighter wire, it lasted almost a half day. The second morning with the new operator carrying the SCR300 on his back, Monk proceeded up to the point where he directed more destroyer fire.

This second day went much better with some of our backup crew helping to crank the generator. Monk had the destroyer firing at a slow pace while our lines were being stabilized as the gap was being closed by Company B of the Seventh Regiment. The second day was a success as the First and the Fifth Regiments crossed the airfield while the Seventh mopped up the south end of Peleliu. Our Third Battalion secured and anchored our lines, as the First and Second Battalions began bumping up against Bloodynose Ridge. They caught heavy fire from the well-fortified Japanese.

Even though the fighting would go on for days, the main objective had been taken on schedule. The Japanese were well entrenched in their coral ridge strongholds, and it was going to be costly in men and material to blast and burn them out.

Early on the second day I had time to go down to the beach where I saw bombs about every four feet sunk into the sand with their noses barely visible. This explained why on the first day I saw a tank get its track blown off trying to crawl up the beach. It is a wonder more tanks and tractors were not damaged with all the explosives waiting to take out anything heavy enough to trigger them.

The second day's temperature was just as hot as the first day's, up to 115 degrees. There was no shade anywhere. I noticed the temperature more on the second day because I was so scared and busy the first day that my mind was not thinking about anything except surviving. I ate well that second evening. My stomach had adjusted and I had calmed down. I was ready for a good night's rest. However, the Japanese had in mind to make one more attempt to dislodge Hunt's Company K.

Hunt was in a better position to fight them off this time. He had set up more machine guns and had been given some badly needed reinforcements. The gap had been plugged by the Seventh Marines Reserve Company B. All the marines had been supplied with plenty of ammo and were ready for this attack, much more than the night before.

Again I woke up late that night when all hell seemed to be breaking loose. The noise seemed almost as loud as the first day but this time was more concentrated up near the point. I did not go back to sleep. The firing finally slacked off by daylight on the third morning. In Hunt's account he said they counted five hundred Japanese killed in front of their lines.

The third morning I had volunteered to replace the radio operator on the SCR300 who had to leave for other duties. That morning there was a marine killed by a sniper right by our battalion CP. Even though the gap had been plugged, there were still snipers around. I worried that the snipers could see our radio antenna and would use that as a target.

It was now my first time to see the point. As I peered inside the concrete block house, where the 47 mm gun was, I could see three Japanese soldiers around the gun. They were burnt to a crisp. They looked like they were still trying to fire the gun. Along the beach were dead marines who never made it much past the water's edge during the landing. Company I had relieved Company K and was moving out. I did not look over in front of the line where most of the dead Japanese were, but did come upon a pile of about twenty, lying about with all their rifles. No one bothered to get the rifles as we followed along behind Company I. Fortunately, they did not meet much resistance as they advanced along the west side of the island. That was a nice surprise. Company K must have wiped out most of the enemy soldiers early that morning.

Monk had picked up a Japanese rifle earlier that day. He handed it to me and told me to keep up with it. I had enough to tote as it was, but I carried it for a while. Later in the morning I got tired and I chunked the rifle.

During the day I had lost my Civil War dagger my dad had sent me, loaned by a dear neighbor back home. I was unhappy about losing the dagger. I did not have a good sheath to carry it in. When I got back home the neighbor never asked me about the dagger. I was ashamed to tell him that I had lost it. Also, I had a .45-caliber pistol that Appenzeller had loaned me that morning. I carried it to lighten my load instead of carrying the carbine. I never knew how he came by it. It was not standard issue for us.

Company I advanced at a pretty good pace, but cautiously. They looked in every pillbox, sometimes throwing a grenade in the opening. Usually, though, they just fired their rifles into the pillbox. Bullets were easier to come by than grenades.

Late that afternoon Monk was busy checking out a possible target for the next day. He told me to go back and fix him a foxhole and to have it ready when he got there. When I got back I found the radio crew had just moved up. They were stacking coral up trying to make do for protection. This was not as good as a foxhole, but since there was no sand, only coral rock, it had to suffice.

I got to talking to some of the fellows and didn't get started on Monk's foxhole. Monk arrived earlier than I expected and asked about his foxhole. I explained that I hadn't got around to it yet. Monk got angry and told me to get around to it. In fact, he broke several of the Ten Commandments while telling me to get around to it. I began gathering up coral rock and, with help from the fellows, fixed Monk the best equivalent to a foxhole I could.

It now was dark, and I decided to forgo a foxhole for myself. I did not think I would need one. Hein said he had a little extra room in his foxhole and invited me to use it. I was hesitant but after Hein insisted, I climbed over the coral he had stacked and lay down with my feet beside his head. The only comment Hein had the next day was that my feet "sure did stink." We slept through the night without much problem, except for Hein suffering from my stinking feet.

On the fourth day, I Company continued up the west side with the ocean on our left. The *New York* battleship, built around 1911, was amazingly close to the beach. Instead of three guns, the older battleships had two 14-inch guns to a turret. I could see the difference between the impact of the 14-inch shells from that of the 5-inch shells from the destroyers. These older battleships were used almost entirely for shore bombardment.

Some of the 14-inch shells hit the beach area about five hundred yards from us. One 2-gun salvo hit something that sent a towering cloud of smoke into the sky. I never knew what caused the thick smoke.

That fourth morning, while in a heavily wooded area, we got hit by some 155 mm shells from our own artillery. The attack was quickly called off. Luckily, no one was hurt. After that, I promised myself I would never stop without digging a foxhole. Being young, I didn't always keep that promise.

The fourth day went well with I Company still moving up the coast. Monk had our radio crew move up to where we were that fourth day. We began to make preparation for the night on a coral bluff about fifteen feet high where the ocean washed up against the bluff. There was hardly any room to walk between the bluff and the ocean. A narrow ravine led down to the beach with just enough room for a man to crawl up to where we were making camp. We had most of the backup radio team, approximately eight marines and two navy men, with us. We were all busy getting places where we could stretch out and sleep for the night.

There was no sand and not much loose coral about with only small scrub trees trying to grow out of cracks in the coral. Everyone got situated fairly well except me. I got caught with not much space. I was located almost in front of the ravine leading down to the beach. Monk was situated almost within arm's reach from me.

It was getting dark when Soto whispered that he heard something below the cliff. We knew no marines would be fooling around down there so someone suggested dropping a couple of grenades. Soto and the fellow near him did not want to do this. They said that they didn't know how many Japanese were down there nor did we know how well armed they might be. Instead of dropping the grenades we posted guards for four-hour shifts.

With the Japanese so close, I hardly slept all night. Just across from us, there was a two-man crew with two black dogs. These dogs never let out a sound all night. They had been trained to stay quiet. The dogs were used to sniff out pillboxes instead of risking a marine for the duty.

Around four in the morning Rommel was on guard duty about fifteen feet from Monk and me. I heard something stirring at the bottom of the ravine. I turned to Monk, shook him quietly, and told him there was a Japanese just below crawling up the ravine. Monk turned back over, muttering that it was just my imagination, that nothing was down there.

I knew there were enemy soldiers down there because I had heard a rifle scrape against the coral sides of the narrow ravine. I could now hear someone grunting as he tried to reach the top of the cliff. I heard his rifle scrape the coral again. I did not dare peep down in the ravine and expose myself. I still had the .45 with five rounds in the clip. I had fired one round the previous day to make sure it would fire. I released the safety, with the Japanese soldier about six feet from me. If he did see me, he may have thought I was a fellow Jap because I still had on the khakis. I yelled, "Who goes there? Who goes there?" He stopped, got quiet, and gave no password. That told me he could not be one of us.

I stuck the .45 straight down into the ravine and squeezed off two shots. I heard him expel air and groan as one of the bullets caught him in the side in the lower part of the stomach. He half fell and slid all the way to the bottom of the ravine. Naturally, everyone woke up. Rommel had never heard a thing. I don't know if he heard me wake Monk up.

By coincidence everything worked to perfection by everyone staying quiet. The dogs never let out a sound. Shortly after I shot the .45, maybe ten minutes, a terrific explosion went off below the cliff. Five minutes later another explosion went off. The Japanese soldier was still alive and trying to do some damage to his enemy before he left this world.

We did not know a marine duck was just around the other side of the cliff. The Japanese soldier was most likely trying to take it out. He apparently did not want to risk throwing the grenade up on the cliff, thinking it might fall back on him.

As daylight came we found his rifle and glove at the bottom of the ravine. Some of us circled around behind the cliff where it sloped down to the ocean. There we found him, lying face down in the water. One of the marines on the duck had been hit by some shrapnel in the leg, but was not seriously wounded. He claimed he had killed the man. I turned the dead Jap over and noticed that he had one large wound in the bottom of his stomach. That was where my .45 bullet caught him. I could tell I had hit him from the groan he let out when the bullet struck him.

The dead Japanese had a small bag containing some very small biscuits. We found a religious keepsake in one of his pockets. Captain Johnson, our navy officer, asked me if he could have it. Of course I said yes. He thanked me and told the others they needed to thank me for saving them. I don't know what Monk thought. He never said anything. By turning back over and trying to go back to sleep, it worked better. The Japanese may have heard us stirring around if Monk had not quietly turned back over.

I took a lot of kidding from the fellows after we got back to Pavuvu. They kept repeating the story that I had not really paused between the "who goes there?" that I had just fired off the two rounds. I must have heard "who goes there? Bang! Bang!" spoken in rapid secession several times.

I have thought a few times how things came together for my benefit, the .45 pistol revolver, the khakis, and the silence. Otherwise, I might not have made it. I don't believe I could have swung the carbine around in position quickly enough to stop the Japanese soldier. I believe God worked these events to our salvation that night. My sister later told me how my dad prayed for me every night while I was in the service. He was a deacon for fifty years in the County Line Baptist Church, seven miles north of Marvell, Arkansas. He lived to be ninety-one years old, passing away in 1984, at my sister's home in Marvell. That morning his pastor had come by to visit him. Dad told the pastor that he did not want to talk, that he had an appointment to keep. I don't have to guess what that appointment was.

The morning that we found the dead Japanese I had shot, Monk remembered the Japanese rifle he told me to take care of. He asked me where it was. I cleared my throat and told him I had gotten tired of carrying it. He was getting ready to bawl me out when I told him if he would give me an hour, I could get him all the rifles that I could carry.

I headed back to where I saw all the dead Japanese soldiers the third morning, praying I was ahead of the souvenir hunters. When I reached the spot none of the rifles had been picked up. I gathered as many as I could carry and headed back to our radio location.

On the way back I ran into three marines looking for souvenirs. They looked me over and asked why I was in khaki. I tried to quickly explain the circumstances. Since most of the Japanese were in khaki and the marines in dungarees, I could have been taken for the enemy from a distance. They asked me where I had found the rifles. I pointed back toward the way I had come and told them they would find plenty of rifles, if no one beat them there. They left and I carried the rifles back to our team's location.

Monk must have been satisfied, he never said anything more to me about it. These rifles were much better than his anyway. We buried the rifles in the sand, intending to come back later and pick them up. Some of our team did go back after we were pulled out and were over in the rest area. Appenzeller was with them and gave my rifle away to a sailor friend who kept begging him for the rifle. I was upset after all the trouble I had gone through to get the rifles. He said the sailor begged him and that he couldn't resist.

Soto, with air liaison, who had been attached to our team, said he wanted to go up to the front and help with the radio. I told him he could take my place if he cleared it with Monk. Monk was the bravest marine I ever knew, but he could be nasty if you didn't do what he ordered. In two days Monk had Soto so frustrated that he was ready to go back to what he had been doing.

Things started slowing down for us about this time. We felt fairly safe behind the lines, but had a guard posted every night. Hein and some of the fellows would sing, harmonizing way into the night each evening beside the beach. We moved in toward the high ridges and the fellows were still singing every night. After our ordeal everybody felt much better, but we now had time to think more about home. We all got pretty lonesome.

The campaign was not over. It just slowed down some for us. The First Regiment was assaulting Bloodynose Ridge and having a rough time rooting out the Japanese in their reinforced defenses. We were just far enough behind the lines that we were not bothered except for a stray shell now and then. On the eighth day Major General Roy S. Geiger had the Eighty-first Army Division's 321st Regiment relieve us. Our First Regiment had suffered so many casualties that they needed to be relieved in order to have enough experienced marines left to rebuild for the next campaign. The First Regiment was not a viable force with 60 percent casualties. The Fifth Regiment fought on twenty-two more days and the Seventh twelve more days.

All the regiments were depleted about the same as the First by the time they were pulled out. Only a small pocket was left for the army's Eighty-first, about 400 by 500 yards. It would take about six more weeks for them to dig the last of the Japanese out. We talked some with the Eighty-first spotting team as they took over our position there in the woods. When we left, they began laying more loose coral, reinforcing our coral protective walls as above-ground foxholes.

We walked out with all our gear to a narrow road where two trucks picked us up and carried us over to the east side of the island, which had been vacated by the Fifth Regiment. On the way over to the other side of Peleliu I saw dead marines covered with ponchos and a couple of dead Japanese soldiers in the middle of the road who had been completely flattened.

Besides our team we had the remnants of one platoon in the two trucks. The area we were now in was heavily wooded, which gave us much respite from the heat. The cooler temperature was much better. We could bathe, shave, brush our teeth, and relax in a needed fashion and write letters home. I had picked up a bad case of diarrhea and was losing weight. I did not get over it until I got aboard ship where a corpsman gave me some pills to clean me out. I lost close to thirty pounds, and wasn't able to gain all my weight back on our diet of dehydrated eggs, dehydrated potatoes, and Spam.

The marines must have had the worst food in the Pacific. I liked the K rations we had in the field better than what we had on Pavuvu. On top of that, our motor pool guys were doing the cooking, which they never learned to do, not that much could be done with the fare anyway. We did get some lamb, jelly, and some fruit similar to crab apples from Australia. The Seabees and the air force had the best food. I concur with one marine's account where he said he got real eggs only five times and that was aboard ship during the Cape Glouster through Okinawa Campaigns.

Other published accounts of Peleliu state the Japanese had an opportunity to do severe damage to the marines of which they did not take advantage. This involved the two-hundred-yard gap between Company K and the Third Battalion's CP. I believe they did not push through because of the fierce resistance of Company K. Another reason was that our naval gunfire team put so much destroyer fire in front of this area that the Japanese never did get adequately organized for the push. This gunfire was directed by

Lieutenant Myers and Major Platt. Due to the twenty-five-foot-high ridge and the tank trap, the Japanese could not get their tanks through. That left only the head-on assault where they crossed the airfield and attempted to ram through at the junction of the First and Fifth Regiments. Thankfully, there was enough firepower at this sector that the Japanese were stopped.

If the Japanese had been able to recognize our weakness in the gap, they could have rammed through without the tanks. They could have hit our flank and rolled straight south taking out the lightly armed beach parties. They would have annihilated us and made it much more costly for the marines and the army later on. If that had happened our team would have been wiped out. The Japanese still had the manpower at that time to do this. During a discussion back on Pavuvu, one of the beach party officers said beach parties did not need to be armed. This would have been one case where they did, at least with some weapon like the carbine that our team carried.

As I look back on the Peleliu action, I am amazed at the commitment and the sacrifice of all the U.S. forces that fought this battle, the cooperation of the marines, the navy, and the army. All had a part to play. They did it with honor and distinction, with many sacrificing their lives for their country. It saddens me as I think of those whose lives were cut short. I know they would have wished to live out their lives to the fullest.

2

PAVUVU AND THE FIRST MARINE DIVISION

We had calm seas on our voyage back to Pavuvu. Major J. E. Morris and Captain Richard Glaeser pulled all of the First ASCO out of the battalions and had a tent area just for us, rather than have the units out with the individual battalions as in combat. The Fourth JASCO was renamed the First ASCO, standing for First Assault Signal Company, maybe to match the First Marine Division. Most of us would rather have been placed with the battalions as detached units. It gave Major Morris better control and command of his company. That meant we could be reacclimated back to a more military disciplined existence. As a result several marines were sent to the brig for disregarding various regulations. A tent with a bob-wire fence served as the brig with a guard to patrol the fence. The men in the brig would josh whoever caught guard duty. Coral rock was used for the tent floors. The streets were paved with coral. I even caught a cold, if you can believe it, after getting sweaty loading the coral and then cooling off too quickly in the breeze riding in the truck back to the tent area. We built all our own heads and set up the kitchen and mess halls using large tents. For recreation we played softball, went swimming in the bay, fished, went to the movies, and played cards. Poker was played for money, and some skillful marines picked up a bit of change this way. This existence was toward the boring. In some ways this was good. We had had about all the excitement we wanted on Peleliu, so there was some healing involved, with of course the writing of letters to loved ones back home and the excitement of mail call. Hardly anyone was interested in picking fights because everyone was ready for a more peaceful existence. Peleliu was not talked about all that much. Most would rather forget about it. Beer issues were, I thought, adequate, with some cokes at times. I was amused at Lieutenant Smith at times. We called him "Smitty." He liked to call out close-order drill, which he was very good at. The forty-five marines in the gunfire group were all PFCs except for one corporal. One time Smitty was drilling us, and he tried very hard to tangle us up. As long as he called the drill commands correctly he couldn't confuse us. He would march us up to a ditch and say halt to the rear march just in time to avoid us going into the ditch. He finally said after calling a halt that individually we looked like crap, but as a platoon marching we looked great. We had been together about eight months and had learned to be confident in our marching, if the orders were given correctly.

Another funny thing happened. It was decided to take our gunfire group out for a field exercise using the compass to travel over a selected route at night. We were to follow directions using one of the glowing dial compasses that could be seen in the dark. It was twilight and we were divided into three-man teams. We were to go, for example, three hundred yards on one bearing while counting our steps, then turn and use another bearing so many yards or steps, then take another bearing for so many steps. If we did everything correctly, we would come out where one of our lieutenants would be waiting. My three-man group was the third to leave. The departures were about five minutes apart. It was difficult holding a bearing by the compass through the heavy jungle growth, stumbling in the dark at times over fallen trees. I was the team leader and held the compass, while one man counted the steps. Our group finally made it out to a trail, which we followed since it matched the last bearing we were given. Pretty soon we came upon the lieutenant waiting for us in a jeep. Only three groups out of fifteen made it out. I think some of the coon and possum hunting back in Arkansas helped me. The other groups got lost and would yell to each other till they were able to congregate down in the jungle growth. They gave up trying to complete the course and spent the night there together. I don't know what the lieutenant thought. He finally gave up and returned to our tent area. The next morning a very sheepish bunch showed up a little after sunup. I had to laugh. It was the best laugh I had experienced in a long time. These fellows were mostly city boys, some from Brooklyn. They said they had a good time telling jokes and singing most of the night around a campfire for light, so they would not be in the dark all night.

Several of the fellows along with Hein decided to get an inflatable boat and try to do a little fishing in one of the bays nearby. They carried a few grenades along to use like dynamite to stun the fish so they could pick them up when they floated to the top of the water. Things were not going badly until one of the fellows began to crack up. After the exploding of the first grenade, something triggered in his brain. He began lobbing grenades, saying we had to stop the Japs. Hein told me that he was very worried. Somebody could have been hurt. They finally were able to calm the fellow down and paddle back to the beach. He may have been in the same duck that got hit when the big blond air liaison fellow was killed. I never dreamed he would crack up. It was not very pleasant trying to guard him the time I caught guard duty where he was detained. In our shore party the first night on Peleliu, a seventeen-year-old kid lost it during the night. He threw a phosphorous smoke grenade, injuring one of the radiomen. I never knew if the radioman recovered. When one of his group visited him aboard the hospital ship, he was stinking badly from his burns. He was upset and put out about it, which anyone could understand. The kid was shot when he would not calm down. There was much regret over this, some saying there were other ways to have dealt with the situation. These were the only two cases of mental breakdowns that I knew about.

It was decided that since there was not much going on that our telephone men should learn the Morse code. It was a volunteer thing for all who wanted to learn it. I had failed the code aptitude test in boot camp. I doubt if I could have succeeded. Luckily for me it had been decided to send about fifteen men down to Guadalcanal for a month of training with assault teams and do some practice setting up radios. Usually the assault would be in company force with artillery and tank support. Live machine-gun and rifle fire was also used in assaulting the defensive site.

After about ten days all our party, except another marine and me, had made it down to Henderson Field, twenty miles away, to enjoy all the benefits of the PX and the availability of ice cream. This marine and I decided to hitchhike to Henderson Field without liberty permission, thinking we would not be missed from camp. We easily caught a ride to Henderson Field. We had looked the place over some and were enjoying eating an ice cream cone, when out of the corner of my eye I spotted something—Lieutenant Smith and Captain Glaeser walking directly our way. I thought they might pass by and not notice us. Lieutenant Smith said later he would not have stopped but he thought Captain Glaeser may have recognized us. Anyway Lieutenant Smith stopped and asked if we had permission to be there. I said we did not, but since everyone else had been there we should get the chance also. Lieutenant Smith answered, "I want you to start back to camp immediately." We did not lose any time getting on the road leading back to camp walking and trying to flag a ride back. Some thirty minutes later, we saw a jeep coming down the road. As it got closer, we could see Captain Glaeser was driving the jeep with Lieutenant Smith sitting beside him in the front seat. Captain Glaeser stopped the jeep and said, "Get in."

We jumped into the rear seat, and Captain Glaeser drove on toward our camp. In a few minutes Captain Glaeser asked, "Men, do you think you could furnish radio communication for an artillery spotter back to a field artillery unit?"

Having confidence in our radiomen, I said, "Sure we can." The next day we were up there with the spotter and one radio with another one back with the 75 mm artillery pieces. Everything went well with our communications and the assault exercise was completed successfully. When we got back to camp and got out of the jeep, with Captain Glaeser driving on down the road, Lieutenant Smith says, "I don't know what to do with you fellows, but since Captain Glaeser did not seem to be upset, I will let you go if you will promise me you will not do this again." We of course promised we would not.

There was a little creek flowing out of the mountains about one mile from our camp. We tied a rope to a limb in a fairly tall tree that was hanging out over the water. We would go down to the creek and swing out over the water letting go of the rope and falling into the rapid-flowing stream. It seemed like a long time before we would come up and get a breath of air, because the heavy current seemed to hold a person under. This was more fun than being stuck on Pavuvu.

We made an excursion or two out in the jungle near the creek. On one of these we ran across two adult natives and one small native boy about twelve years old. The smaller adult had bad teeth but could speak English fairly well. He would talk about how he had helped the marines locate some of the Japanese. The older fellow also had bad teeth and did not say much. He was holding a small rooster. I suspect that the rooster may have been slated for the pot. The boy had a small pointed pole that he was at times throwing into the edge of a small pool beside the creek, trying to spear a fish. He would look intently into the water, which was not real clear, and would suddenly cast the pole very expertly, it seemed, at something in the water. He did finally spear a small fish.

One day four of us decided to make a more extended excursion out into the jungle to look for bananas and pineapples. We carried our carbines and knives. We left out from the spot where we had been swimming in the creek. We had not taken a compass along. I don't believe we had one. We began walking deeper into the jungle where we found small banana trees with very small bananas. It seemed the natives had picked the fruit as it had ripened. We found only one pineapple that was ripe enough to eat. I cut it loose with my knife and took it with me. Once I believe we heard a wild pig, but did not see it as it rushed off into the brush. After walking about two miles, we thought we should be coming out to a road or trail where we could circle back to where we had come from. We kept going with everything looking very strange. Finally we stopped and realized we were lost. At this time a discussion ensued about the best way to find our way back out. One marine wanted to follow an empty slew back to the creek. I finally convinced them to follow the sun, knowing the sun would set in the west. We kept walking along through the jungle and reached our creek. We had been in there about four hours. I wrote home about my experience, and somehow word of mouth, as it usually does, got distorted. When one of my classmates, Jessie Carr, heard about it back home, the story was that I was lost in the jungle and it was not known if I would be found. The first time she saw my sisters, she asked about me, and my sisters explained that I was only temporarily lost.

I noticed how black the volcanic soil was on Guadalcanal. The thick cane-like grass grew over head high and was difficult to walk through. I also observed that there were fields of vegetables and watermelons the army was cultivating. I also noticed there was a guard on each field. This must have been the richest soil that I had ever seen. The month went by quickly and we regretted having to head back to Pavuvu and the First Marine Division.

About two hundred of us had been assembled along a sandy beach to await an LCI (landing craft infantry) to pick us up. The LCI was late, and with nothing to eat, we began cutting open coconuts that had fallen from the trees just in from the beach, drinking the juice first. After what seemed to be a three-hour wait the LCI nosed into the beach close enough for us to wade out to it. By the time we reached Pavuvu, it was dark. As I remember we were given some K rations to stave off our hunger.

After getting back to Pavuvu, we received some replacements, new fellows who had just come in from the States. I could tell they were so excited because that first evening some of them kept talking way into the night. I could understand because I remembered my first night on Pavuvu, the excitement of being in a new military setting and wondering what the future would hold. Next they would be getting to know the men in the First ASCO. They turned out to be a welcome bunch of fellows. We knew our days were numbered on Pavuvu when we heard talk about a new campaign we were to embark on. The new recruits were merged into our unit with no difficulty and were accepted by all of us older men (as now we considered ourselves seasoned veterans). These new fellows, as would be expected, had questions about combat. We did not try to snow them, but tried to explain to the best of our ability what to expect.

3

OKINAWA: THE LAST BATTLE

It was now time to leave Pavuvu behind, never to see it again. We began getting ready to head for Okinawa. This time we loaded up everything, including our jeep and air liaison's radio jeep along with all our motor pool trucks. I now had a decent pair of shoes and a new pair of dungarees and my same old carbine. The bluing on the barrel had been rubbed away to where the steel was exposed, and it was necessary to keep the barrel oiled to prevent it from rusting. We had the same packs and the same radio transmitter that replaced the one lost on Peleliu. We did away with the telephone and had SCR300s for communication between the spotter and to our main radio transmitter, with the same hand-cranked generator for transmitter power. We had our same team less Gann, who never made it back to us. We heard he had recovered and was doing OK. Our new scout was Quintinela. He was of Spanish and Mexican descent. A new navy officer for liaison with the ships was assigned to our group.

Not long after we got back to Pavuvu from Peleliu, we had a parade on the small drill field to honor the marines who had won medals for valor. Lieutenant Monk Myers received the Silver Star, and four other marines received the Bronze Star. We stood at

LANDING PLAN - 1 APRIL 1945
HAGUSHI BEACHES

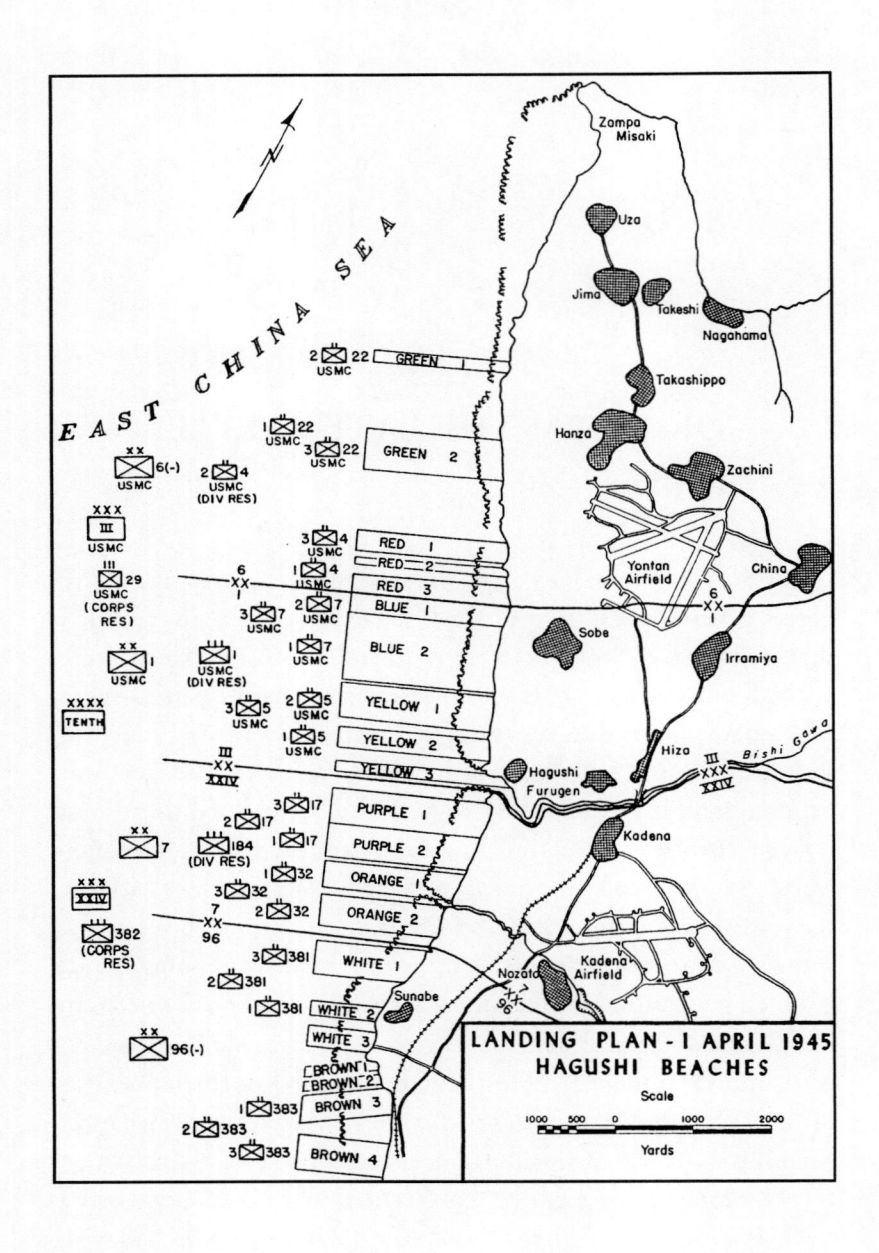

A battleship of the fleet cuts loose with a broadside as she lashes Japanese installations on Okinawa in support of the marine landings on the island. *USMC photo.*

This marine anti-tank gun crew was prepared for a first-rate battle when they hit the Okinawa beach, but they can't seem to understand how they got ashore without firing a single round. *USMC photo.*

attention while the medals were handed out. This was after passing in marching review. The marines who observed us said we looked good keeping in step as we passed in front of the ones receiving medals, looking to the right. I could tell Monk was really proud as he received his medal. He was a well-built blond-headed fellow, six feet tall and weighing about one hundred and eighty pounds. He would have made a good photo for promoting the Marine Corps for enlistments.

This time we boarded a Liberty transport-type ship for the voyage up to Okinawa. Again our crew or team had at its core Monk the spotter; Hein and Klein, the radiomen; with Rommel and me as the telephone men, except we would not be using telephones; and Quintinella filled in the scout position. There were four other new men along to help as needed. One was Hediger, a blond-headed sturdy-built fellow. We finally got underway and became part of a convoy headed for Okinawa. We were a little excited but seemed not to have any particular anxieties about what lay ahead. We stopped off at Ulithi for a final grouping before sailing for Okinawa. A large number of marines went ashore for a big beer party. Since I did not drink beer, I did not go. The ones who went said they had a good time. It was a good break for the fellows before sailing away.

Now there was a huge armada headed to Okinawa, all kinds of troop ships, navy fighting ships, and aircraft carriers. Most of us expected fierce resistance during the beach landings and assault. I remember only one serious alarm of a Japanese air attack. This was about 8:00 P.M. when we were told to get below deck. Some of the men began joking about it, and one fairly young officer told them to shut up. He said, "There really is a bunch of Japanese planes headed our way." Everyone did get quiet, but after the alert was lifted some thought the officer was just a little nervous. We were told that the beach assault would be on April 1. We could hardly believe it when we were told our battalion would be in

U.S. Marines calmly walk out of their landing craft and wade ashore onto a beach that shows no sign of the Japanese garrison on the island. This was a deceiving introduction to a campaign that required bitter fighting later on before the marines could rest. *USMC photo.*

Twilight air attack with the navy throwing up heavy antiaircraft barrage. *U.S. Navy photo of Okinawa air attack, courtesy Nimitz Museum.*

Marines hurdle a stone wall as they participate in a drive across Okinawa. *USMC photo.*

Following the assault troops that hit the Okinawa beach, landing craft disgorge tons of supplies for use in the drive across the island. *USMC photo.*

reserve. Actually, all of the First Regiment was in reserve. I suppose because the First Regiment caught it so badly on Peleliu that first day. It was now March 31, D-1. I don't remember having the apprehension as on Peleliu.

Our ship was sitting farther out to sea than the ones with troops that would be in the first waves. We kind of hung around a nearby radio operated by a sailor. Suddenly a smoke screen was laid down as the assault force headed toward the beach. The assault was scheduled for 0830 hours. The navy had been doing a softening-up bombardment before the landing. Because the smoke screen now hid the beach and landing from our ship position, a very anxious bunch of marines waited to hear how the landings were going. It came as a welcome surprise when we heard a voice over the radio say, "There is no resistance, the landing is going great." Then we heard there were no casualties, only one marine broke his foot on the ramp door of a landing craft. The best I can remember, around 1:00 P.M. the marine companies began climbing down the nets to the landing craft below. It was much later in the day before we were told to get ready to leave. In fact we did not leave the ship till almost dark. Someone jokingly said we must be the Ninety-ninth wave. It turned cool in the late afternoon. Our team was told to get all our communication gear together and proceed to the Higgins boat, an LCP. By the time we were all loaded and in the landing craft it was dark. As we plowed along toward the beach, the LCP slammed against the waves and splashed cold water on me as I was up in bow of the craft. It was very uncomfortable. I was getting cold. One marine really complained. He was not your typical sailor or marine, and he was later sent back to the rear because he was not much help in the field.

It had now become very dark. All at once we heard the sound of aircraft, and tracers began to light up the sky. I have never seen a more beautiful display of fireworks. Tracers seemed to be

Armored amphibious tractors of a marine battalion form into line as the first waves of the marine invaders commence the charge for the beach at Okinawa. *USMC photo.*

Marines hit Blue Beach #2 on Okinawa. *USMC photo.*

crossing the black sky from every ship in the vicinity. This continued for what seemed like at least fifteen minutes. Our officers, realizing we would not have an opportunity to find a place to stay on the beach, decided to pull up beside an LST and spend the night and wait until the next morning to get to the beach. We climbed aboard the LST and found all the troops had disembarked. We had plenty of bunks with room to spare. I slept soundly till the following morning. The LST cooks gave us a hardy breakfast. We got back in the LCP and completed our trip to the beach near the Yontan Airfield. With no particular duties we walked around, not going far, just looking over the site.

Later in the afternoon but before dark, I was standing directly behind a 40 mm antiaircraft gun manned by three marines. I saw a single wing plane starting to circle over the airfield. I could see it had fixed landing gear. It looked like a Piper Cub, only much larger. As it got even with us at about fifteen hundred feet elevation the marines began firing their antiaircraft gun. I could see tracers coming close to the plane. It looked like the last shell may have hit the plane. The kamikaze pilot was now over the beach and headed out to the sea where our ships were. The ships opened up. The plane glided on through the barrage and appeared to hit a battleship in the distance. We later heard that it was the *New Mexico*, and the plane had hit a gun turret, killing some sailors.

Several times I saw the navy put up a barrage using five-inch guns to reach high in the sky. I did not know that the five-inch guns could be used this way, and later read where the navy had developed special fuses for this. Once a navy fighter plane flying low over the beach had to wag his wings to show he was friendly to keep from getting shot down. He escaped with his own navy firing at him. There wasn't much in the way of antiaircraft fire on land. It was entirely different out at the sea. With the ships clustered together they could put up an almost impenetrable barrage.

The navy used destroyers for picket duty on the fleet's

perimeter several miles out. This was to give an alert to the main fleet. They had fifty-five destroyers damaged or sunk while exposed with no supporting fire. It was a lonely vigil with only the individual ship's guns for protection. This had to be unpleasant duty. One time I remember listening to Tokyo Rose when she was describing the kamikazes to the sailors and marines, saying you cannot escape these suicide planes. For the most part the marines considered Tokyo Rose to be an entertaining radio personality, and there was some truth in her description of the kamikaze planes.

One evening someone had found a guitar that had the small "e" string missing. I found a piece of telephone wire and removed one of the steel strands. You see, wire used for field telephones had four steel strands and three copper strands, steel for strength and copper for conductivity. After some difficulty I managed to tune the guitar. I sang a few songs strumming the guitar, making chords to match the melody. Any little diversion was welcome for the men.

From April 1 to April 30, we had a somewhat peaceful existence. The army and the Sixth Marines were doing all the heavy fighting. The First Marines had swept across the island to the eastern shore. After that the First did mostly search duty of interdicting the few Japanese troops that had been stranded about the island. The First did help the Sixth Marines on the north end of the island, looking for bypassed troops.

About the third day we relocated beside a road not far from Yontan Airfield. We began to see some of the first Okinawan natives being taken away to secure camps. On this day we found a small rooster. After killing it and picking off the feathers, someone made a spit from some small tree limbs so the chicken could be roasted. A fire was built under the spit and soon the rooster was roasting. This was working rather well when a group of native Okinawans came along escorted by the military police to a detention camp. There were children in the group and they began pointing to the chicken we were roasting. I thought maybe this chicken could be a pet or maybe they thought we were just mean to be eating their chicken. We were amused at the children talking among themselves while pointing at us. It was so different from my other experiences that the memory has stayed with me for over fifty years.

Monk began to take us on search excursions for any Japanese soldiers who might be hiding among the civilian population. On one of these there was a young male who appeared to be about seventeen at a farmhouse with a group of children and older civilians. I felt like this kid should be left alone. This place had not been touched by the activity in the area. The folks seemed to be going calmly about their daily activities and lives. Anyway, Monk did not want to take a chance on the fellow and decided to apprehend him, taking him to a detention compound. He willingly came along and did not seem to be particularly disturbed by being snatched from his idyllic setting. At the detention center the guards were a little rough with this fellow, according to a member who took him there.

Being from a farm in Arkansas, I naturally began to notice that the Okinawan farms were very small. The predominant crops seemed to be sweet potatoes and sorghum. Since their planting season had not started I could not tell for sure. With the war going on there was not going to be much planting. Normalcy would be returning sooner up on the northern end of the island where the Sixth Marines had finished their campaign in one month.

Okinawans were small in stature, with the women being bigger than most of the men, it seemed. When you saw them the women would be carrying the heavier loads and the smaller men would be trudging along carrying less, behind the women. I was amused at this and got some idea about the lifestyle of these people, at least on their small farms. It was not an easy life, but it did seem to be a peaceful one with only the bare necessities. Later I read where this was the first time war had come to these shores. The land was poor but would have grown good crops if fertilizer had been available. I remembered there was not much commercial fertilizer being used at that time back in Arkansas. The land in Arkansas had not been tilled as long, however, and had not lost so much fertility.

At the Yontan Airfield the runways were rapidly being cleared, repaired, and made ready for aircraft to land. The first airplane that I saw land was a big C-154 four-engine transport plane. A small group of nurses were aboard. They brought their own tent in which they would live temporarily. It did pass through my mind that this was not the most efficient way to ship tents. Even the support pole was included. There were a number of heavily damaged Japanese aircraft along the length of the airfield.

While we were on the edge of the Yontan Airfield, there was an amusing little incident between Monk and Smitty, the air liaison lieutenant. Monk's jeep had not been unloaded, but Smitty's radio jeep *had* been unloaded. Smitty's air liaison team would get to use their jeep much more than we would ours throughout the campaign. They had the back-carried radios like we did. It may have been the greater distance with the aircraft carriers being farther out to sea than the destroyers. I never saw our jeep until about a third of the way through the campaign. Anyway, Monk wanted to borrow Smitty's jeep to look more extensively around the area of the big airfield. Smitty did not want to loan Monk their radio jeep, which I could understand. Monk begged Smitty to let him use the jeep. Smitty still would not relent. So Monk says, "I am getting in this jeep and I will return it in about one hour." Smitty remarked, "Major Morris will be very unhappy when I tell him about this," as Monk drove off in the jeep, leaving Smitty in a cloud of dust. True to his word, Monk came back in about one hour. We hardly used our jeep during the campaign. A few times we hauled our radio gear in it. Much of the terrain was not suitable for the jeep. During the time at the southern part of the island when all the roads and hills were so sodden, one gunfire team found a horse that they used to haul around some of their gear. The horse finally floundered and could not go on. They joked about the horse giving up, but the marines had to go on anyway. Actually, the horse was probably not getting the feed it needed.

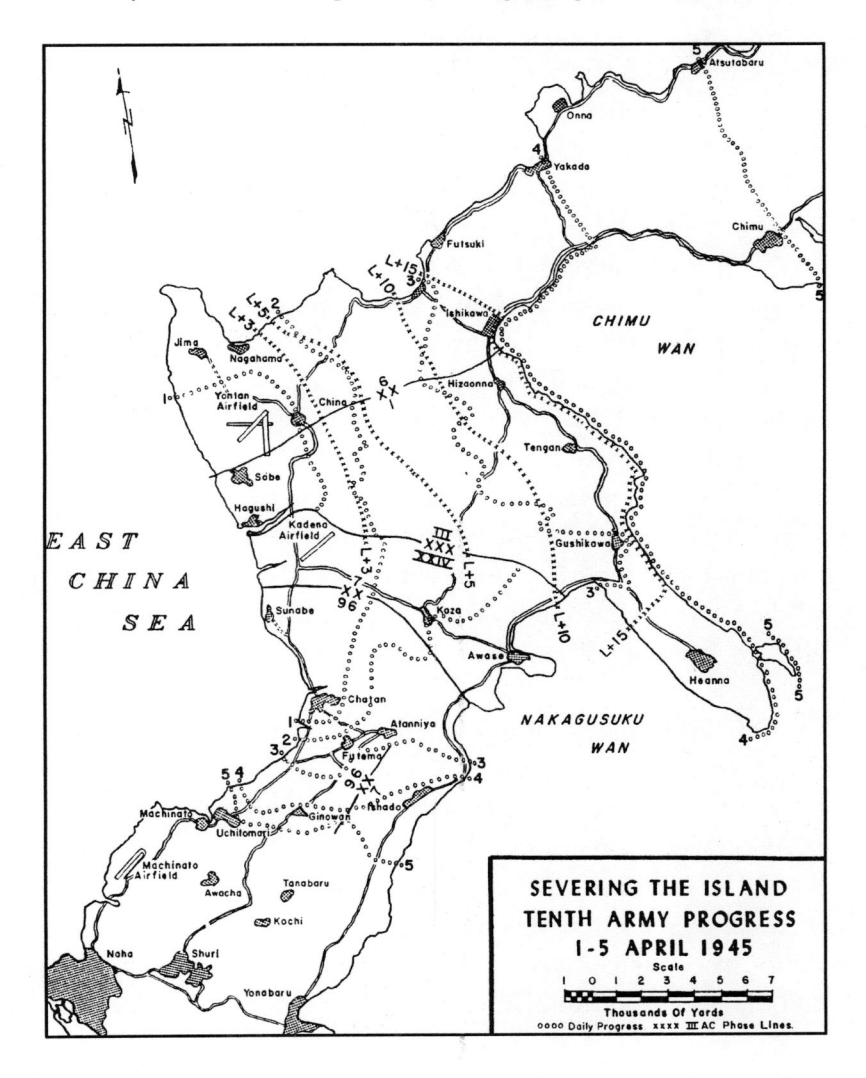

OKINAWA: THE LAST BATTLE 75

One night during the first week when we were about one-third of the way across the island, east of the airfield, a few Japanese soldiers bumped into one of our companies. They may have been trying to reach their comrades to the south. This company of marines kept up extensive firing and did kill some of them. Then, they began to run short of ammunition. A squad from the company came up to the headquarter's company that we were with to get any ammunition that could be spared. They were given most of what could be found. It seemed to me these marines just wanted to work off some of their frustration from not getting to see much action up until that night. I'll bet their officers made sure they had a better supply of ammunition and made sure they did not fire up so much ammo unnecessarily.

We were about six days into the campaign when we were told to get ready to move north to help the Sixth Marines do some searching for bypassed Japanese. The Sixth was moving much faster than expected. They had swept up into the northern part of the island, and the First had swept across the island to the east coast. The Seventh and Ninety-sixth Army Divisions had driven down to the first preplanned defense line the Japanese had set up across the island. I would not have wanted to be anywhere near the southern part of the island the first month. The Japanese had all their forces intact and a huge number of gun emplacements well stocked with ammunition. They would fight to the bitter end.

Our Third Battalion headquarters and two companies were loaded into 10x10 trucks and traveled about forty miles to near the north end of Okinawa. It seemed like we were up there about ten days. Monk had our six-man team going out on patrols almost every day. We never saw a single Japanese soldier. On the trip up there we passed through very beautiful country, somewhat hilly. In one place I remember a hill, more like a small mountain, that had the most beautiful flat terraces all the way to the top. I have never seen anything more striking in my life. The first day our battalion unloaded beside a calm, scenic ocean cove. Several of us couldn't resist the opportunity. We stripped off our dungarees and enjoyed a fantastic evening of swimming. This was a beautiful and peaceful setting, in stark contrast to all the villages we saw destroyed on the way north.

The next morning, just after a breakfast of K rations, I heard a peculiar noise to the north. There was in the distance a plane, just a speck in the sky, coming toward us over the hills. I spoke to one of my buddies, saying, "That plane sure sounds different from ours." It has been said by others that some of the Japanese planes sounded like an old-style washing machine. As the plane approached I grew curious and kept my eye on it. Still thinking it might be one of ours I was surprised when a solid red painted sun could be seen on the side of the fuselage with two Japanese pilots in the plane very visible with flight caps on their heads with the goggles resting on their foreheads. They just glanced down toward us, appearing to be very calm. The plane looked similar to one of our navy torpedo planes with a plexiglass canopy. The colonel's body guard jumped on a .50-caliber machine gun mounted on a truck and began swinging it around to fire on the plane. Colonel Sabol shouted loudly over to him, saying, "Stop, don't fire! We have too many men out here in the open. I don't want to give him any excuse to strafe." There were over two hundred marines in the open area. Our naval gunfire and air liaison teams got on their radios to warn our division down south. I never knew what happened to the plane. I believe this was an observation plane looking the situation over for the Japanese. I'll never forget how nonchalantly they had looked us over sitting one behind the other in their seats as they flew away.

It was nice duty up in the northern part of Okinawa. On one of our patrols, we had climbed to a heavily wooded area that looked very dark and forbidding. I did not know if Monk was going to have us check it out or not. I was pleased when Monk said, "I don't believe we should go any further." I had a feeling that something was in there. We were lightly armed with carbines. After we got back to camp, the word was given that we would be returning back to the south near the Kedena airfield. We were transported back in trucks.

I was amazed at all the activity that was going on to improve the airfields. There Rommel had me help him gather boards of scrap from destroyed buildings to put together sort of a hovel-type shelter with more room than the two-man pup tents. Rommel was good at improvising. He was a machinist from Indiana. We mostly spent our time brewing coffee or chocolate and preparing meals and relaxing. Our fare was mostly K rations with a few cans of stew or meat, which we would heat up using wood scraps or sticks. We even used the explosive C compound, which was safe, because it had to have a detonator to make it explode. One night we were alarmed when some Japanese bombers flew down from Japan and dropped a few bombs in the distance. Luckily, these were not close to us.

There was one instance when a plane loaded with about twenty-five Japanese landed right on the edge of Yontan Airfield in a two-engine plane. They jumped out and began blowing up planes parked along the runway. Some cooks got into action and helped to subdue them. My wife's brother was one of the cooks. He told about it after the war. I never heard him say he had actually killed any of the enemy. Things went along rather well for our team until we were told to get ready to relieve the Twenty-seventh Army's Infantry Division that had been shot to pieces by the massive barrages from the elaborate Japanese artillery emplacements facing them. We were to shortly find out just how bad it was.

We were even kind of excited at first. We believed we would really move forward against the Japanese. We made sure all our radio gear had fresh batteries and was ready to use. We traveled part way in trucks. We unloaded our gear and backpacks some distance from the front to prevent making the trucks a target. We then marched near to where the Third Battalion, First Marine headquarters was setting up behind the front lines. There was an army spotting team for naval gunfire similar to ours there that we were relieving. Shell holes were all around where we were setting up for the evening. We arrived about 3:00 P.M. I asked the army officer in charge of their spotting team why all the shell holes were there. He said, "You will find out about five o'clock." This was not what I wanted to hear. I could tell they were anxious to get out of there and were greatly appreciative of being relieved. Sure enough, large shells began arriving about 5:00 P.M. There was a low terraced embankment in front of where we were setting up. This furnished some protection. I did not know, then, that the Japanese could observe what was going on from where they were on higher ground. This was obvious later when we had advanced and could look back on this site. For some reason I dug my foxhole on top of the embankment instead of below it. Our 81 mm mortars were being positioned behind us off to our left as we faced south toward the Japanese lines. Again, as on Peleliu, my appetite was lacking that evening of the first day of action. Most of the others did not seem to be affected this way. The sun had set and the shelling had slacked off a bit. I suppose the Japanese liked to interrupt our meals. About 8:00 P.M. a Japanese soldier crept through our lines and sent a flare rocket up some 150 feet directly behind our location. It looked like the color of one shot from a roman candle we used to fire at Christmas time. Immediately we began receiving heavy shelling. None of us was touched. I was lying in my foxhole about midnight, when I decided I needed to get some sleep. The shelling was still going on, but not as heavy. I prayed, "Lord, I am going to get some sleep. Please take care of me." I peacefully fell asleep, dreaming of home. During the night a Japanese infiltrator got within about seventy-five feet south of my foxhole. Fortunately, he was discovered by some headquarter marines just to the south of me. The Jap was wounded in the exchange of fire. Rather than surrendering, he blew himself up with a grenade. He was close enough that Monk asked me the next morning if I had killed him. I replied, "No, Monk, I was sound asleep and did not hear a thing." Maybe the Lord did answer my prayer, after all. Monk may have been remembering the Peleliu incident.

On the morning of the second day, May 1, 1945, Monk wanted to get started to the front lines and get in some licks using our naval gunfire team. We checked the SCR300s to make sure they were receiving and transmitting properly before Monk left. Rommel took one of these units for Monk to use and the other would be left at our main radio site near the battalion CP. The first day when we began receiving the artillery pasting from the Japanese, I really felt sorry for the headquarters master sergeant. It would not be overstating to say our team had gained a great deal of confidence from our Third Battalion in our ability to counter some of the Japanese fire while on Peleliu. The sergeant began saying, "Naval gunfire, can't you stop some of this and get us some relief from this stuff coming in?" I knew that in this situation we were not going to have much luck stopping the Japanese artillery. Some of the Japanese artillery was located in caves with rails extending through the cave opening, allowing the guns to be rolled out. After being fired several times the guns could be rolled back inside. I will say our navy high-velocity guns were more effective than the lobbing artillery for shooting into the caves whenever they were discovered. Monk told the sergeant that he would do all he could. Monk was told to be very selective and conservative in choosing the targets. This word had been passed down from the higher commanders in the navy that these shells had to come a long way across the Pacific. By then it was known that this would be a long campaign. At the start Monk did try to be efficient in his target selection. If a good target of opportunity presented itself, Monk could use his own judgement. Monk and two men, Rommel and Quintinella, reached the front lines and began calling in target coordinates, with the usual firing of a minimum number of rounds to get on target. Back behind us setting off to our left, as I stated earlier, the 81 mm mortars were located on a small three-foot rise. They used a spotter for their fire direction also.

The second day the mortar squad began dropping rounds down the tubes with the objective of supporting the marines on the front lines. The mortars must have been giving the Japanese some pain and concern, because immediately the 81 mm mortars began receiving artillery shells near their emplacement. Our radio team was just far enough off to the side that we were not bothered, except to feel sorry for the mortar squad. The mortar squad had to stop firing for a while, but every time they would start firing the mortars, the Japanese would send some more artillery in on them. This back-and-forth exchange went on most of the day with the mortar squad taking casualties. Finally the 81s were not fired unless the companies were desperate for support. During the time we were at this location every time replacement troops or whole relief companies would be moving through the area, the Japanese shelling would start again. It was obvious to me the Japanese had our location zeroed in, using their observation point somewhere inside their lines. The marines used very little camouflaging on Okinawa. This site was so out in the open that camouflaging would not have helped much.

The best location for mortars was behind a hill, where the mortars could be fired over the hill and the hill would give protection to the mortar squad hiding the emplacement from the Japanese. I remember vividly later on when the 81s were located behind a hill, while I was over to the side, about seventy feet away,

I was watching this same crew drop the rounds down the mortar tubes and seeing the slight smoke from mortars as the projectiles rose over the hill at about a forty-five-degree angle. They would fire all four mortars at the same time. This position was safe enough that I felt no concern being so close to this crew. Mortar fire can be very effective and very demoralizing, as was demonstrated to me that first day on Peleliu soon after landing, especially if caught out in the open as we were on Peleliu. The Japanese were usually well entrenched in their fortifications. There were times when they would be exposed while launching an attack on our lines. There is one exception to the safe-behind-a-hill theory. That is, if the mortar is located close enough to the target where it can be elevated to high enough angle that the projectile will come in almost straight down and can hit the reverse side slope of the hill.

During the first part of the Okinawa campaign it seemed to me that the Japanese had more artillery than we did. The Japanese had large stocks of shells of every kind. It was not long, however, until this situation changed. With the Eleventh Marine Artillery and the Twenty-seventh Army Artillery, which were left in place after their infantry was relieved, adequate support was provided. As the campaign wore on I was astounded to witness the artillery units as they sent the most terrific time-on-target barrages.

The first few days it seemed to me as if our battalion did not move more than a thousand yards and appeared stalled. It became a dual between the two opposing forces, with artillery, machine guns, rifles, and mortars on each side slugging it out.

Monk was frustrated because he wanted to do more. He fumed under the restrictions placed on him. On Peleliu, he practically had a free hand. As I have stated earlier we had gained respect for naval gunfire support.

There was one small incident on about the third night after getting down south. Hediger and I caught guard duty to watch for infiltrators. We were located in a large shell hole out to the right of our radio location. We were getting shelled by a lone Japanese gun. The shells were landing off to our left, more toward the 81 mortar position, again. Hediger and I were not particularly anxious until shrapnel started zinging by now and then. By keeping our heads down we seemed not to be in much danger. I noticed that Hediger was becoming a little nervous. Realizing that this was his first action, I said, "Hediger, why don't you go behind the embankment and stay in your foxhole. I can take care of this duty OK. If I need you, I'll come over and get you. There is no need for both of us to be out here." Hediger was pleased with my suggestion and left for the more secure location behind the embankment. After that first night we knew someone would have to be on guard at night. The Japanese were excellent at sneaking in and catching anyone not alert.

My main job was to keep our spotter supplied with batteries. About every two days I had to carry a battery up to Monk. He would be at the front line or at times in front of the line. I remember one time I took a battery up for the SCR300. I approached where Monk was located, and saw the most unshaven and haggard bunch of marines I had ever seen. They were resigned to their fate, whether it was life or death. You could see it in their eyes. The company was located behind a small hill, which gave little protection. They had made the deepest penetration and were waiting for the other companies to move even with them. The first time we went up there it was very quiet. Rommel and I had gone over the left side of the hill looking for Monk. A valley running east to west lay below us. No firing was taking place. Nothing was stirring and it was peaceful even though we knew there were Japanese hidden across the valley. If they saw us, they were in no mood to fire. Perhaps they were eating supper. I asked Rommel, "Are we in front of our lines?" He answered, "Yes, we are." We talked only a minute or so and casually climbed back over the hill where we found Monk. It was late in the evening and darkness was nearing. I told Monk I had better head on back. He replied, "Homer, don't come up here by yourself anymore. It is too risky. If you get hit, you should not be alone." I believe Monk by then recognized that I was not a coward, even though he may have had doubts on Peleliu, when I was not able to reach him due to sniper fire.

On the way back from the front lines, not far from Monk's position, I saw a clump that I could not identify. On looking closer, I could see it was a dead marine. There was not much left of him. I said to myself, "You poor fellow, you were coming up as a replacement and never made it." I had seen so many dead marines that it did not get to me that much. I had mentioned previously that the Japanese liked to sneak in at night and catch anyone posted alone on watch. The very next time I made the trip up with Hediger, four marines were just then bringing back one marine who had been posted on guard duty by himself, just a short distance in front of the line. They were carrying him in a poncho, holding on to the four corners. One marine nearby asked if he was dead. One of the four replied, "Yes, he's gone." He was a small young fellow. This did depress me. I wondered about him and about how the Jap was able to sneak up on him in the night. And just how scared and lonely he must have been to be posted out in front of the lines.

On another of my trips Hediger was carrying a spare battery and I had a replacement SCR300 strapped to my back to replace one that had been riddled with shrapnel. Our radio repair group back in the rear echelon had previously sent word for us to take better care of our equipment. We wondered what they thought when they saw this radio damage. As Hediger and I came up to the top of the last hill with a small grassy valley to cross to reach Monk's position, we met a squad of marines who had been throwing smoke grenades to hide anyone going down the hill before crossing the valley. Snipers had been harassing and picking off marines at this spot. The marines there threw a couple of smoke grenades to hide us also. As we left the protection of the smoke I broke into a run and did not slow down till I reached our destination. One marine said, "Man, you were sure making good time coming across there." I said, "I wasn't going to let any bullets catch me." Hediger had lagged behind me, doing a slow trot. When he reached me, he complained that I had run off and left him. I wasn't bothered the least bit by his comment.

One other time the company on this same hill had asked for some air support to keep the Japanese in check. I had to take Smitty, our battalion air liaison officer, up to this hill so he could call in the air strike. Smitty wanted to observe the strike through a forty-foot opening in the west side of the hill. Monk informed Smitty that he should use another spot since a sniper had picked off a marine there that morning. Smitty was determined to observe from this spot. Monk decided that he would stand by with him while the strike was being observed. Both were of equal rank. Smitty called in the strafing and bombing runs that had been requested. No sniper activity occurred. Neither Smitty nor Monk was going to let the other appear to be braver.

The only place the company could go was down in the valley below the hill. The exposure was just too great there. The Japanese were on the ridge across the valley. Until a full-scale attack could be made, this company had to stay in place. This time when Quintinella and I went over the hill to look around a bullet zinged right by us. We jumped in a foxhole, but every time we would raise up above the top of the foxhole, a bullet would pass over us. I yelled, "Quintinella, how are we going to get out of here?" He said, "I'll scramble out real fast and if I make it you wait a minute or so and do the same." We did not hear any more bullets whistling by as we crossed back to the other side of the hill.

After we had sat back in our original position for about a week, the battalion CP was moved up closer to the front because of the advance made by the marines. This helped our radio communication, because of the shorter distance between our sets. As we moved up I didn't think the Japanese could see our advance. We had stayed out of their view until we rounded a hill and crossed a small valley with a ditch in the middle. Just as we crossed the ditch, they began lobbing what appeared to be 75 mm artillery shells. We quickly moved right to the edge of the hill. I became concerned because the hill had such a slight slope that the shells were dropping near the edge of the hill. Smitty's air liaison team had not crossed the ditch. It appeared that they were going to get hit. They began to scramble around trying to dodge the shells. They finally made it across the ditch without getting a scratch. I believe there was only one gun firing, which improved their chances. I was amazed that no one was hit.

The next morning Hediger and I decided to go pick up some gear that had been left in our jeep from the day before. This was the first time our jeep had become available to us. It was parked behind the hill from the way we had come the previous day. On the southeast side of this hill was a 75 mm howitzer. The marines had stopped firing it because the Japanese had it in full view and would shell it whenever it was fired. Realizing that the Japanese did not like to see any activity around this gun, I said to Hediger, "Let's circle around the hill the way we came yesterday." Hediger said, "No, let's go straight up the hill. We can reach the jeep quicker. "Naw, Hediger, I don't like this way, the Japanese might see us," I argued. Not wanting to appear yellow to a new recruit I finally agreed to start up the hill. About a quarter way to the top, we heard the whistling sound of a shell coming. It exploded about eighty feet behind us, just after we hit the deck, not catching any of it. Hediger wanted to lie down and wait out the shelling. After not wishing to just lie there I jumped up and yelled, "Let's keep going! Run as fast as you can, and hit the deck when you hear the shell coming in!" This we did. When we heard a shell whistling we would hit the deck and get up after it exploded. Finally we had gotten almost to the top of the hill. By then the shells were just over to the side. It seemed like the next one just might get us. The Japanese gunner was very good. He was tracking us up the hill making slight changes in his gun elevation. I glanced over to my left and was amazed to see a small cave entrance. We ducked inside while a few more shells came in. This was the only time I ever shook from a scare. I said to Hediger, "I don't believe I am a brave man." I promised to myself, "I'll never let anyone out talk me again." Hediger and I came very close to getting it. The gun was moved from that location the following night, back toward the rear. I told Hediger, "You can go back this way if you want, but this fellow will circle around by the side of the hill." After picking up our gear, we did circle around the northeast side of the hill on the way back. There was no more shelling. When we arrived safely back to our radio location, I asked one of the fellows if he saw us almost get clobbered. He said, "Yes," but didn't seem very interested in our close call. Hardly a day went by down on the south end of Okinawa that we did not get shelled. It was amazing that none of our team had been hit yet.

The big shells the Japanese threw at us the first few days had been about 50 percent duds. I saw these big shells go scooting across the ground, but not exploding. If these duds hit anyone, however, it was goodbye. (I now realize these shells were fired from high-velocity guns, which was the reason the trajectory was so flat, not directly impacting the detonator in many cases.) This saved many marines and army troops. Early one morning I really felt for a bunch of replacements who were moving up to the front. Of course the Japanese had seen them and had opened up with their big stuff. The shells came streaking right into the midst of the fellows. They had spread out enough that I don't remember

B Company moves up in push that was later captioned "Death Valley" because of the more than 125 casualties in eight hours while crossing the draw. *USMC photo.*

Men of the First Marine Division keep close to the ground while under heavy Jap mortar and machine-gun fire on the crest of the newly won hill bounding "Awacha Pocket" on the Naha front. The marines sealed off the pocket in the three days of bitter fighting and killed more than one thousand Japs. *USMC photo.*

anyone getting hit, at least by the duds, but some of the exploding shells may have caught some with shrapnel. Again, we were just a little way off to the side and no rounds fell on us. This is not to say the Japanese never did damage with their shelling. I heard an officer call in to the CP and tell the battalion commander his company was catching heavy shelling. He said his men were almost out of their minds, and he did not see how they could take much more. It was just too much. The commander said he would try to get them some artillery support. I believe he said they could shift to a more secure spot if there was a hill or ridge close by.

By May 18 we had moved up one more time and the First Marine Division was advancing. This was good news until suddenly word came through that Rommel was wounded and Monk was killed. This was the most shocking news of the war for me. Our entire team was affected. We were just so sad over it. I thought that Monk was invincible and that nothing could ever stop him. We couldn't just take off to see him. We had our duties to perform. I believe Hein was given permission to go see him. One of our shore party marines got to see him. He remarked that Monk, in death, had the same expression as in life. His mouth was clinched and his jaw set, as if he was ready to take out a few more Japs. I did not try to see him. I wanted to remember him as the vibrant and active person he was. We were informed that Monk and Rommel were trying to get a lone Jap soldier when the Jap managed to throw a grenade in on them. Rommel caught shrapnel in the neck and Monk was killed. Rommel must have made sure it was over for Monk before leaving him. Rommel was able to get to the rear where he was taken to a hospital. He recovered and was sent back to the States. Monk was probably carried a short distance by stretcher, then placed on a treaded carryall that could negotiate the terrain to the marine cemetery. In my opinion Monk and Rommel should never have tried to get the Jap by themselves. They should have waited and let a more experienced squad take the Jap on. Nothing is more dangerous than a cornered Jap. They always seemed to have grenades hanging on their belts.

Monk had a good pair of binoculars and was always searching for a target from his spotting position on the front lines and some of the time in front of the lines. He was very aggressive in not letting a good target go without calling in fire on it by a destroyer or larger ship, even a crusier or a battleship if warranted.

Two new officers were sent to take over Monk's duties and replace our liaison officer. Both were navy officers. The navy spotter was a small thin fellow. The fellows with him at the front said he was just as motivated as Monk. While directing fire for a destroyer, he got his helmet creased by a Jap sniper. The liaison officer was thirty-six years old and had participated in the Normandy invasion in France. He was involved in scuttling some ships to provide an enclosed harbor for shipping protection. For some reason he had taken a liking to me. One evening I had been picking up boxes of rations from an air drop and was late getting back. He saved me a can of pork and beans, something that I liked so well.

After being pulled out of the lines for two days we moved back toward the front to take up new positions. One of our new replacements was complaining about not feeling well. I encouraged him to hang on till we reached our new position. We located behind a hill with a valley to our north. I dug a foxhole in the side of the hill big enough for two men. This fellow was still suffering. He went over to the battalion CP where a corpsman gave him some pills. The next morning he was so stiff that he could barely walk. I helped him over to the CP by letting him lean on me as we walked slowly to get there. The corpsman had him sent directly back to a rear hospital. The first report we received stated that he was not doing well. Then, shortly, the next report said he had died. What we did not realize was that he was having an appendicitis attack. His appendix must have ruptured, and the hospital did not get to operate in time. I have always blamed myself for not getting him the attention he needed. I just did not realize how ill he was and neither did the corpsman that first evening. He might have been saved if he had gotten the attention he needed. This had us all depressed for several days. The war went on, but now I knew there are more ways to die than from bullets

At this same location I relaxed in my nice safe foxhole in the side of the hill. It was actually the best foxhole I ever had. Suddenly four navy aircraft came straight down the valley letting go with their .50-caliber guns in a strafing run. I was about even with their elevation above the valley floor. Klein said, "Someone get on the radio and report this." These fighter planes appeared to be flying at top speed. The air liasion group got on their radio and reported the situation back to their command point. The pilots, no doubt, thought they were over enemy territory and were trying to help out. I was in no danger tucked away in my foxhole. Our battalion didn't use the air liaison team as much as the naval gunfire team. One reason is because it is much more difficult for pilots to discern between enemy troops and friendly troops. This problem is still being worked on till this day.

About June 6 down at our battalion's southernmost approach to the south end of Okinawa, we had spliced in our lines to those of the army's Seventy-seventh Division. One of their division's air liaison teams had called a marine air wing to make a supporting air strike for them on a hill just in front of their lines. This four-plane wing got mixed up and mistakenly took our hill as their target. I heard these planes approaching flying at about one thousand feet. I thought they would fly on over our location, when all at once the lead plane peeled off and began diving directly toward us. I said, "Something is wrong!" The plane let go two rockets, which hit and exploded very close to us. The next two planes fired their rockets, also, which struck farther away. The last plane dropped a bomb. The only thing that saved us was their failure to strafe. We still had about ten marines injured. None of our group was hit. This was the most helpless feeling I ever felt on Okinawa. I thought, "I don't like being killed by the enemy, but by one's own forces is just too much." Again our air liaison jumped on the radio, but the attack was over so quickly the danger had passed. These two strikes by our own aircraft were the only instances of friendly fire that happened to our team during the war, except for the 155 mm barrage from our artillery on Peleliu.

All our forces were making advances and loosening the Japanese defenses close to Shuri Castle. I had gone over to an adjoining naval gunfire team, for what reason I have now forgotten. One of their team had picked up an '03 rifle that had a scope mounted on it. He said, "Look through the scope and tell me what you think." I was amazed how sharp things looked through the scope. He said, "I am told a man can be killed a thousand yards away by this rifle." That is slightly more than one-half mile. This was the only '03 I had seen. The marines were apparently using the '03 on rare occasions. While I was there I watched an eleven-man marine attack squad in the valley below following a tank advance against a Japanese position. It was a courageous action to observe. I thought, even with the tank, I would not want to be down there with them.

When the two new navy officers took over our team after Monk was killed, Hein decided that he wanted to see some action up at the front with the new navy spotter and Rosenbloom, who was newly assigned to replace Rommel. We called him Rosey. The new navy spotter was a very nervy fellow. He began to concentrate more on the caves because the naval guns, with their high velocity and straighter trajectory, could better cope with cave openings than the lobbing howitzer artillery. The naval ship would ask for a more detailed account of their gunfire. Rosey being on the radio to relay the report back, while not making false claims, would enhance the reports and was a little more creative than I thought necessary. In the past our reports were very factual without any shade of enhancement. Rosey's reports would say how the caves were completely sealed off and the shells had made direct hits with devastating effect. Naturally, this got the navy crews more enthused and they were responding with increasing effort and interest. These reports of Rosey's were very vivid, and, of course, the ships personnel appreciated it. This went on for maybe two or three days. Actually, this probably was our most effective gunfire of the campaign on Okinawa. Finally, Hein caught a few pieces of shrapnel in his rear, which was not bad enough to take him out of action. An injury report was made, and he later received a Purple Heart. This left me being the only one out of our original six-man team to not get a scratch in battle. The new navy spotter was calling in more gunfire than Monk had been, except when he was on Peleliu. I knew the navy wanted the Okinawan thing to be over, especially the destroyer crews that were facing the kamikaze planes out on perimeter picket duty. I believe our naval gunfire greatly helped, and it was not long until the combined effect of the artillery, the bombing, the heavy rains, the mud, and the army and marine assaults began to take a terrific toll on the Japanese defenders. The Japanese had fired most of their ammo. There was no resupply for them. The situation was changing rapidly to our favor.

As the Japanese defenses were crumbling, the enemy began to retreat and leave their unburied dead and the knocked-out tanks and guns. The weather took a turn for the better and three of us decided to go toward the front to see what souvenirs we could find. We came up to a small hill that was really more like a knoll and spotted a Japanese tank half buried in a way that the gun could still be operated. It was destroyed. As I looked back to the rear, I could see that the Japanese could observe much of our activity on the lower hills from where we had come. I thought that the gun on the tank may have been the one firing at Hediger and me. On this hill were at least thirty dead Japanese. It looked like they may have been caught by an artillery barrage, since they were lying so close together. Just on the other side of the hill was a cave that had a one-cylinder gas engine connected to a generator. There were several Japanese rifles stacked inside the cave. One rifle was supporting a tarp to shield a piece of radio equipment where water had been dripping down from the top of the cave. We proceeded to gather up the better rifles. I stupidly picked up two Japanese grenades and hung them on the back of my belt. When we had returned back to our radio position, the navy liaison officer said, "Homer, I want you to dig a hole immediately and bury those grenades. You could get hurt and maybe hurt someone else with the nasty things." He, being a wise old thirty-six, had much better judgment than a nineteen-year-old. I ordinarily did not pull such a stupid stunt.

It had been raining off and on for several days. On this day there was a heavy overcast, and the sky was very dark from the cloud cover. It was May 26. We just happened to have our radio receiver on when we heard a spotter in a plane. He sounded excited, "I see about five hundred Japanese soldiers moving south. I'm going to call in some naval gunfire on these Japs." We listened as he proceeded to direct the fire on this bunch of troops caught out in the open. Later on I saw the result of this carnage as we were leaving the Shuri Castle area. One marine picked up a sword off a dead Japanese officer. Our navy liaison officer remarked, "I am not surprised since the weather gave them some cover." It seems there was a break in the clouds and it was a coincidence that the spotter discovered them. This meant that the Japanese were retreating from the originally strong Shuri Castle fortified defenses that now no longer existed. For us the attack had been going on for twenty-six days and for the army a month more.

Marines on Sugar Loaf Ridge. The army spent six days trying to take King's Hill and the marines spent three days taking the same. Sugar Loaf Ridge is the highest point next to King's Hill. *USMC photo.*

Scene near the front lines. *USMC photo.*

The back of the Japanese resistance was broken, and we were moving out. We approached what had been the main defense line at the Shuri Castle area. As we marched along an incline that led up into the Shuri Castle ridge line, we began receiving shells from a lone high-velocity gun. The shells zoomed over the top of the ridge line, which kept them from dropping down on us. Nevertheless, we could hear the shells exploding back to our rear. The shells were probably five-inch and coming from the southwest. Their closeness disturbed me, as well as a platoon of marines led by an officer who was encouraging them along. I can still see in my mind the marine officer talking to his obedient troops, telling them not to worry, the ridge line would prevent the shells from striking them. Pretty soon the shelling stopped. The scuttlebutt was that the shells had been coming from one of our ships. If it was our ship, it was firing most likely at some retreating Japanese. I never knew, but was glad when the shelling stopped. That afternoon we set up in the middle of the Shuri Castle area. I thought we would get to stay there awhile. Along about 2:00 A.M. we were awakened and told to get our gear together, that we would be moving out under the cover of darkness. At the time, I did not know the reason for this. I was later to find out that our overall command wanted us to race down and beat the retreating Japanese to the Kunishi ridge. That would be their last major defense line. The army was ahead of us over to our left. We marched all morning and until about 3:00 P.M. We did not stop to eat. There a parachute supply drop was made by our marine air wing. We had out-run our source of supply. We were now in contact with the Seventy-seventh Army Division. Their men were older than our marines. Some of them came over and helped us gather the supplies. They even shared some of their food and water with us. After we had gathered up the supplies, we began getting a few air bursts from the Japanese artillery that I had never seen before. Luckily the bursts were not over us or there would have been casualties. The air bursts were exploding to the north. We did not get hit. As dusk approached, a squad of marines came over the hill carrying a badly wounded marine. They had run into some retreating Japanese who were trying to delay our advance.

At this juncture with the Seventy-seventh, it had been raining earlier and the ground was wet. I did not dig a foxhole but spread out the bag that contained our radio antenna sections. Believe it or not, I did not remove the antenna rods. I lay down on the bag to keep my back off the wet ground. I slept soundly enough, then the next morning we were told to move out again. After eating breakfast and telling the army fellows "so long and thanks for the food," we were on our way.

This is when I recognized that the army had a much better supply system. One of the army soldiers told me they had never been supplied by air drops. Actually the Marine Air Corps did make some air drops to the army. I read this in another account of Okinawa. The marines could perform large army-type operations, but their logistics of supply was not as developed as the army's. The marines had trained for beach assaults and small island-type fighting where there were generally no long supply lines. One of my early school-day friends, H. L. Blevens, my age, was in the navy. He had landed both marines and soldiers by landing craft on Guam. He said the marines were trained to rush off the craft, while the soldiers were more hesitant and slower leaving the craft. The marines had much more training for landing assaults than the army. The marines had perfected this type of assault using amphibious tractors that could navigate water or land. The landing craft were used more for the landing of the later waves.

We had gotten underway, traveling on foot farther south. We proceeded on till we came to an open field with a small ditch running through it, but surrounded by low rises. At this spot a lone Jap sniper began to take pot shots at us. Our officers said, "Keep

A marine in a fire fight with a sniper. *USMC photo.*

moving." The bullets zinged by, which made me uncomfortable, but not very nervous. We kept going until we were out of range of this Jap. No one was hit. He must have been the poorest shot in the Japanese army. Shortly after this we angled into the lines of the Seventy-seventh Division and marched along where a good number of their troops were alongside the road embankment watching us. We walked along inside of their lines for quite a ways. This kind of hurt our pride, at least mine, using the army for protection. I swallowed my pride, knowing we were bypassing some Japanese that other marines would have to deal with later.

The strategy was to get our battalion down there fast and help secure the Seventy-seventh Army's right flank. From east to west the line up was the Seventh, Ninety-sixth, and Seventy-seventh Army Divisions, the First and Sixth Marine Divisions, all strung across the southern end of Okinawa.

We proceeded on to a small hill about one thousand yards in front of the ridge the Japanese were defending. Behind the hill we were safe from a 47 mm high-velocity rifle that was pestering the area. The sound of the shell exploding was heard before the whistling of the shell moving through the air got to our ears. With lobbing artillery shells the whistling of the incoming round is heard first. The rise in elevation of the hill protected us from this gun. There was an empty house not yet destroyed just behind the hill. This is where our team spent the night, joining the officers. Our spotter had tried to spot the gun just before dark that evening, but had no luck. The next morning the gun got a lucky hit on an ammo dump inside the Seventy-seventh lines. The dump was too close to the front lines. Shells began to explode. All day the ammo in the dump kept exploding. There was just enough heat from small fires to cause the shells to explode, which would then set off another shell. A road curved around the dump. When jeeps came along by the dump, the driver would speed up.

Two new officers had been put in charge of our team. Our

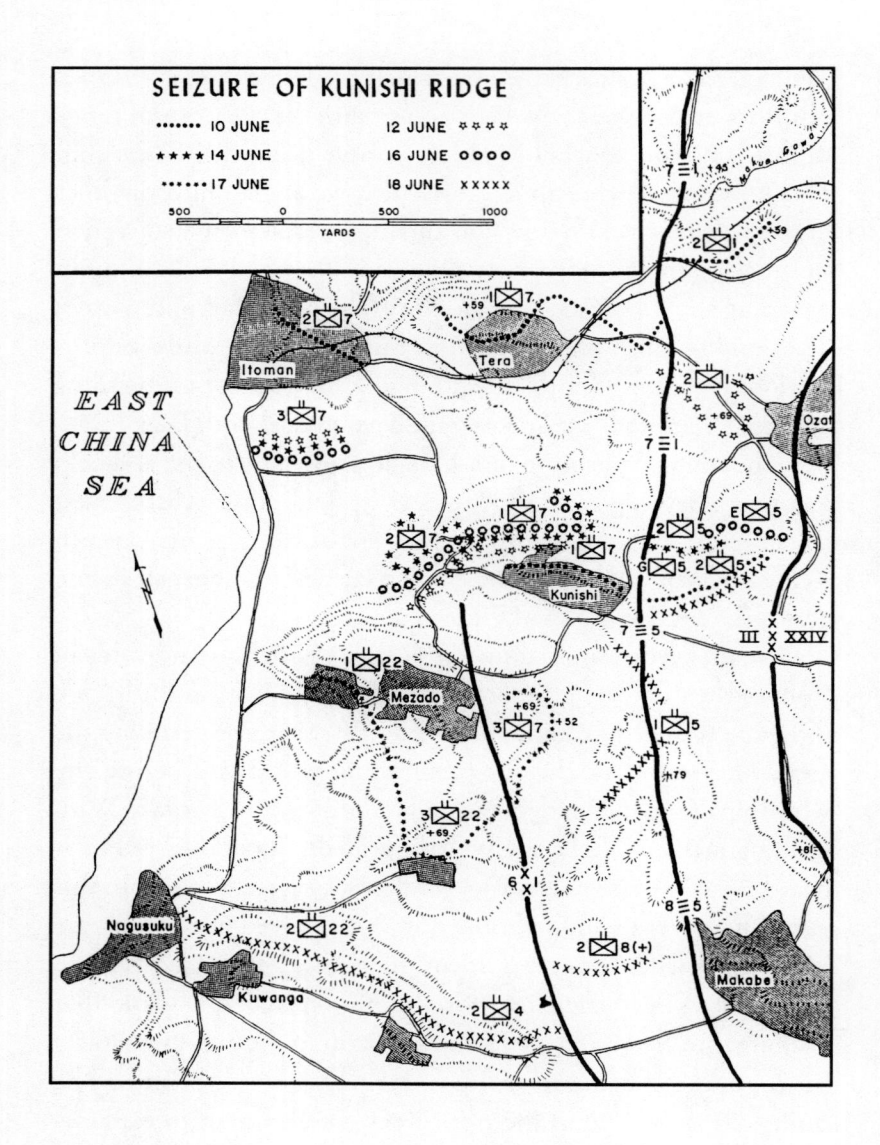

battalion was in reserve quite a bit, and we did not do much spotting for naval gunfire. I was with our two officers when they called in our last gunfire support. We had a good spot on top of a small hill. The marine company took their objective, with only two marines wounded.

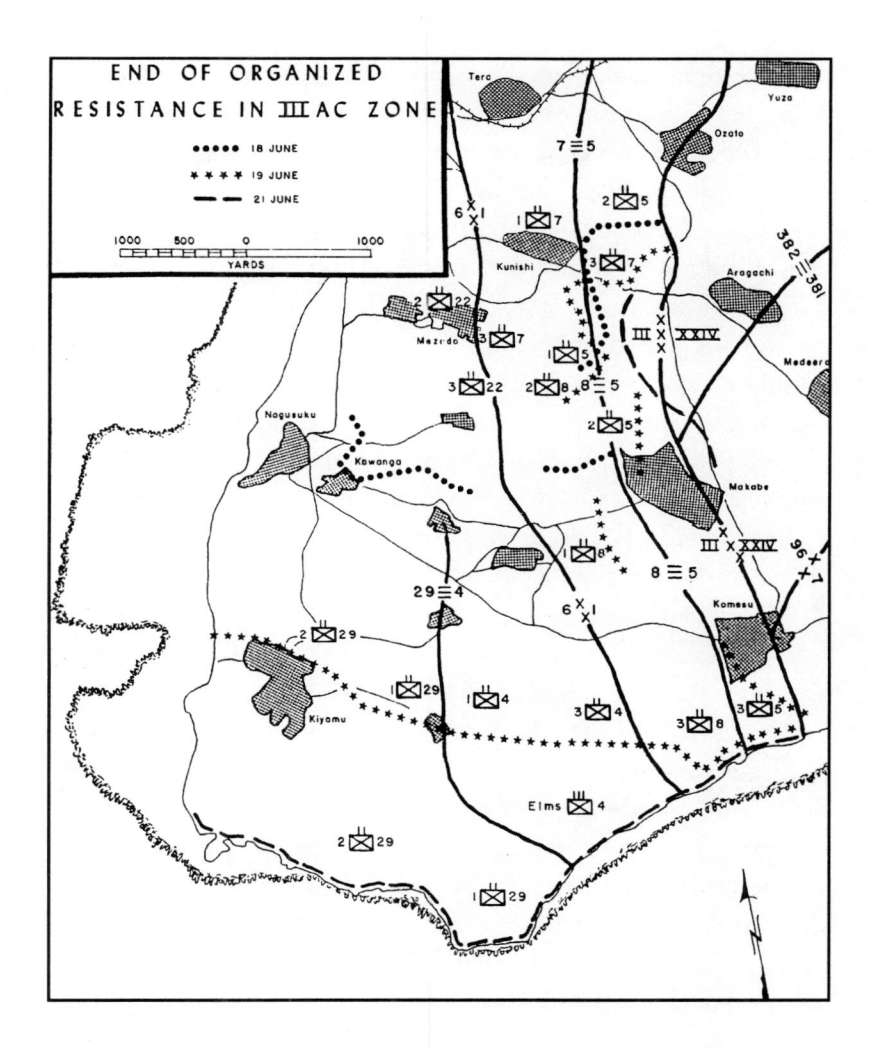

It was the last of June when the order came for us to march back north and set up south of the Yontan Airfield. As we came into the area, a Jap straggler was hiding in a small clump of bushes. A marine rifleman was passing close by when this Jap, armed with a pistol, jumped out of the bushes and plugged the marine in the forehead, killing him. The Jap did not last but a few seconds as several marines converged on the spot mowing him down. I heard the shot fired by the Jap. The next thing I saw were the marines firing into the clump of bushes where the Jap had retreated. Our team began to check all the small caves in our area. I fired into one, emptying my carbine clip. There were no Japs in the cave to my knowledge, even though I thought I heard something stirring in it. I did not go in to investigate.

We set up camp in the area. That night, I had never heard so much wild firing in my life, most of it coming from the Seabees and the service troops. It sounded like a small war going on. There were a few Jap stragglers about, but it seemed these troops were more nervous than they should have been. Maybe they were just having a little fun. One night at an outdoor movie, the movie had to be stopped because there was too much firing into our area. While at this location, again at a movie, I felt one of the tremors that these islands are known for. The quake gave me a very uneasy, unstable feeling. The screen was really shaking, and I wished the shaking would stop. It was a relief when it did.

We got word that the First ASCO would be together once again, bivouacked in an area on the west coast of Okinawa, four miles north of Yontan Airfield. When our team arrived most of the tents had been put up. I suppose the shore parties were released from their battalion duties earlier than us and had done most of the work getting the site ready. The mess hall was complete. The top consisted of hugh tarps placed over some rafters supported by poles. This was a beautiful location near a fifty-foot cliff. There was a path leading down to the ocean. The beach was sandy with rocks large enough to scrub and wash cloths on scattered about all along the beach. I went swimming there several times. The tent area as usual was arranged in neat rows. Each tent was allowed one 60-watt bulb. The electric power was supplied by a couple of gas-driven generators. At first telephone cable was used for the power supply, but the wire had too much voltage drop. We strung some heavier cable, which remedied the problem. Our team was together again; Hein, Klein, two new fellows, and myself, all sharing the same tent.

Out of all the rifles we had picked up earlier, only one beat-up weapon was left. This was the one that Rommel had found early in the campaign. The other Jap rifles were stolen one night out of our jeep that had been left behind when we marched south after the Shuri Castle line was broken. I asked Klein one day while we were sitting in our tent, "Why don't we crate up this last rifle and ship it to Rommel in the States?" Klein agreed with me. After finding Rommel's address, we shipped the Jap rifle to him. We were lucky to have gotten his address.

After the move to the spot by the cliff on the west coast of Okinawa, we stayed there until we left for China. On August 8 we heard about the A-bomb that was dropped on Japan. I could not believe it at first. We did not celebrate much. We heard that the Twenty-seventh Army Division, located south of us, celebrated in a big way, firing rifles into the air. We were close enough to them that we could hear some of the gunfire. This was the division that had been shot up badly down south during the first month of the battle.

There was one entertaining event that took place. Every day for several days about 2:00 P.M. a marine Corsair plane would fly over and buzz the camp. It would dive down at a terrific speed and pull out of the dive just past our tent area. The pilot would usually repeat this two times before he flew away. I never knew who was doing this. It may have been one of our air liaison officers, who thought it might help morale. I appreciated this bit of flying demonstration. The F-4 marine Corsair was known to the Japs as the "Whistling Death." I was glad the pilot was on our side.

The weather on Okinawa was pleasant in late summer, but as I remember, a hurricane hit in early September of that year. The top of our mess hall was blown away. The tents held up well, except for one flap that was not secured properly. I observed that this hurricane behaved as hurricanes do. The winds reversed after the calm eye with no wind passed through. The ships at sea had a rough time as would be expected. One small craft was blown on to the beach below the cliff. It looked like a big luxury fishing vessel or maybe a small Coast Guard craft. I was surprised to see this type of craft in the waters near Okinawa.

Our officers built themselves a nice clubhouse just north of our tent area. There was always a guard walking this area, guarding the officers' tent area and our enlisted men's tent area. I caught guard duty some of the time for these areas. At night we could hear the officers carrying on like a bunch of college kids, singing and making a lot of noise. Our enlisted men were more restrained. Our sergeants would not have let us cut up that much. Most of our recreation consisted of going to the movies, playing cards or softball, writing letters home, and going swimming down below the cliff. It was a very relaxing time after all we had been through. There were the usual beer issues. Whenever there was a beer issue, there would be several small beer parties.

Before the big bomb was dropped, preparation for the invasion of Japan was being planned. With the surrender of Japan, there was no more need. We had been worried about the casualties that we knew would occur. Now we were greatly relieved. Some of the older men were being sent home. I never did get down to the Yontan Airfield to look around again. We begin to hear about the point system that would determine when a person would be sent home. The older men with the most service time had the most points.

Our food was still dehydrated eggs, dehydrated potatoes, and Spam. We may have gotten a little more meat and vegetables. I didn't gain much weight. It was good to just be alive.

In early September we got word that the First Marine Division was going to North China. I would have liked it better had we been going home. I had not been home in two years. Now this trip to China would take us farther away. This is one trip I don't remember much about. I don't remember getting aboard the troop ship that would take us to North China. On the way we saw several floating mines. They were destroyed by gunfire from destroyers. This trip was similar to others. Again the food was better than we had been used to; there were fried eggs, which were a welcome change from dehydrated eggs.

Our ship dropped anchor off Tangu, which was about thirty miles from Tientsin, China. I would be in China for another five months.

4

CHINA DUTY

Our voyage from Okinawa to North China had been uneventful when our ship anchored off Tangu, a small town on the North China coast. A small river, Hai Ho, ran from Tientsin to Tangu. Some of the smaller landing craft were able to navigate the river, but to get us into Tangu, LCTs were used. Marines used LCTs to land trucks and tanks through the open hull of the ship by doors that could be opened. It was smaller than the better-known LST, which could carry a larger complement of tanks and men. We were off-loaded from our transport into the LCT. We climbed down nets to the flat bottom of the LCT. Our craft entered the mouth of the river about dusk dark. While our craft navigated the river, Proctor, one of my buddies, and I went below to the engine room. We were amazed at how clean and polished the engine room appeared. The big double-opposed piston engine was pounding merrily away. When I saw there was hardly a speck of grease on the engine, my respect for the navy was enhanced. They must have put great store in maintaining the engines in their fleet. We went back topside. The craft maintained a midstream position by going forward and floating backward then forward again. Shortly, a Chinese man appeared at the side of the craft with a pint of whiskey for sale, "Price one American dollar." I don't remember anyone taking him up on the offer. It amazed me how he reached the side of the railing from his small craft below. It was not long until the LCT docked, and we debarked. I felt mighty strange in a strange land, and I did not know what to expect.

After leaving the LCT, we marched a short distance to an empty building where we began preparing to spend the night. I suppose arrangements had previously been made for us to occupy the building. I still had my carbine slung over my shoulder by the strap, and I was in no hurry to set it down. Hein said, "Homer, we are among friends." I kind of had my doubts, but set the carbine aside. Everyone else had set his carbine down, and I did not want to appear ridiculous. The next day we moved to an abandoned military school building where we stayed for almost two months. Next door was a small independent local military unit who we watched marching every day. In the distance a lattice of canals crisscrossed to allow ocean water at high tide to flood the sandy plain. The gates would be closed to retain the ocean water. Then, the salty sea water was left to stand until the water had evaporated, leaving the valuable salt. The salt and some small amount of sand was scraped off and placed in boats for removal to a dumping site before being shipped to a processing center.

Our cooks began buying some beef at local markets. This beef had not been refrigerated. The beef I saw was purchased in half sections. It had an unpleasant smell, yet, after being cut up and cooked, it tasted all right. We located some hot plates that operated on 200 volts, 25 cycles, which also serviced the building. We bought eggs at outdoor markets in town for ten cents a dozen and cooked them using the electric hot plates. Our work schedule was light, which gave us extra time do things for ourselves.

The building already had a large telephone switchboard, which we placed in service. One circuit was connected to a forty-drop board that the marines had installed near the dock at Tangu. A young Chinese lad who stayed around our barracks a lot helped put the building switchboard in service. He was a very sharp and knowledgeable lad, about eighteen years old.

I had to stand watch some on the marine switchboard in Tangu, but we had enough telephone men that I did not catch it very often. One day while taking care of the calls on the Tangu switchboard, I accidently disconnected a navy officer who was talking to someone up in Tientsin. He started cursing. I tried to mollify him, but he would not listen and continued cursing. I plugged his drop back into the Tientsin circuit. Luckily the line held and he started talking to his party again. From then on I was little more careful. Actually, this was the first forty-drop switchboard I had worked. The field switchboards were mostly twelve- and twenty-drop units, with which I was more familiar.

While we were at Tangu, we were allowed to go up to Tientsin on liberty. The thirty-mile ride in a 10x10 truck was over the roughest road I have ever traveled. It had a pitted gravel surface and many deep potholes. It was a jarring ride in the back of the truck. Tientsin, however, was a modern city by Asian standards. I would place it more like an American city of the 1920s. It had streetcars, streetlights, and electricity. Most of the buildings were a dull gray, but some had brick construction. There were no bright colors; there were nightclubs for entertainment and restaurants. There was one bazaar five floors high with a large open space in the center clear to the roof. You could find almost anything from cameras to rings.

I went to one nightclub that had a small four-man band of Filipinos with stringed instruments. Every night they would sing "South of the Border Down Mexico Way." This touched me because it was so popular in the thirties and early forties in the States. The musicians must have gotten stranded there during the war. At one French restaurant I had pie a la mode. The restaurants originally served beer, but it did not last long with all the thirsty marines around. Fortunately, the marines had their beer issues to fall back on. There were all kinds of mixed drinks available in the nightclubs. In fact, the girls in the nightclubs would drink the pink nonalcoholic beverage while the marines would drink the stronger mixed drinks. These girls were there to dance with the marines, entertain them, and sell more drinks. Most of the time, the clubs that I went to had a full house, but were not overly crowded. At the first nightclub I visited, one of the girls took an interest in me. It was about ten days before I got back to Tientsin. She told me she cried when I didn't show up. I explained that we were located in Tangu and didn't get to Tientsin very often. Every time I showed up there, she would come over and sit at my table. She was about the best-looking girl in the club. I didn't understand what she saw in me. Not knowing much English she would say, "You are so pretty." I had to take all this with a grain of salt, so to speak. One fellow said, "Homer, you sure know how to pick them." I took her out to a small restaurant, where I ordered a hamburger. She had me to order her a Chinese dish, which she ate using chopsticks. She tried to show me how to use the chopsticks, but I just couldn't pick up the food this way. One time I took her shopping, and we rode in separate rickshaws. These had the front wheel the same as a bicycle, two bicycle-type rear wheels, a seat for the passenger, and a little top like a buggy. The pedals were the same as a bicycle. There must have been hundreds of rickshaws in Tientsin. The girl bought a few things, and I paid for a pair of socks she wanted. Somehow I lost track of her, and then saw her one last time in a different club. She was dancing with a marine I knew, and I didn't try to cut in. I did tell the marine he was dancing with my girlfriend. What I did not know then that was many of these girls were helping to support their families.

At one club I got acquainted with a Korean girl and took her out to a restaurant. She knew very little English. We had ordered our meal and were about half done eating, when she motioned to a waiter to come over to our table. She began talking to him in Chinese, and I did not know what they were talking about. The waiter left but came back shortly and explained to me their conversation. He said the girl told him she was supporting her family and wanted him to find out if I would give her some extra money. I said, "Sure." I was sorry I had only three dollars in my billfold. I gave her that, and she seemed to relax and looked pleased. I had sent most of my money home to my folks. I sure wished I had kept more of it. Thinking back to that long-ago time, I still feel sorry that I couldn't help her more.

I did buy a few things to take home. I bought about ten pair of silk stockings that were not available back home. I gave these to my mother and my aunt and some of their friends. I bought a string of cultured pearls for eight dollars from a jewelry store operated by a Russian lady. These were appraised back in the States at a value of two hundred dollars.

We went to Tientsin about every two weeks. One late afternoon we were getting ready to travel back to Tangu by truck when we were told to take some rifles along because some Communists were roaming the countryside. We were handed mostly carbines as we loaded into the lone truck to make the trip back. I did have a slight bit of anxiety. We stopped about halfway to Tangu at a house right by the road where a very old Chinese man was sitting outside smoking his pipe. One of the marines asked him if there were any Communists around, using mostly sign language. He indicated there were none around. We proceeded on our way without sighting anyone who acted like Communists. I was glad when we reached our barracks in Tangu. The marines were assigned the task of repatriating the Japanese back to Japan. While the Nationalists were favored, the orders to the marines were to stay neutral between the Nationalists and the Communists. The

U.S. State Department was not sure about its policies. Some thought the Communists were only agrarian reformers. Many found it hard to know for sure who were the good guys. There was no clear-cut decision. I remember this back in '42 when I was a high school senior. My opinion is that our State Department failed on this and maybe were misled by some Communist sympathizers in the department. While in North China I was concerned that the marines might get involved in a conflict and cause our stay there to be much longer. What we really did was delay the conflict to a later time, when we should have nipped the bud when we had the opportunity. We may have lost 10,000 men rather than the 37,000 later on in Korea. The bad thing about that is that I might have been one of the 10,000. I imagine it would have been hard to sell this back in the States. We were prepared to expend a half million men in Japan before the A-bomb. Why didn't we expend a small fraction of that to get rid of the problem then? There were another 50,000 sacrificed in Vietnam; that might also have been avoided.

Along about November 1, our ASCO group moved from Tangu to Tientsin to some former Japanese barracks. These were nice quarters with about six men to a large room. We slept on cots. Each room had a coal-fired stove for heating. The pile of coal outside on the grounds was a very low grade coal. Some of it was part shale or rock. Each marine chipped in fifty cents a week for a Chinese boy to pick out the good coal and keep the stove filled enough to provide adequate heating. He did a good job on this.

We went on liberty more often at Tientsin. Guard duty was rotated around for the barracks and the motor pool, one mile away. Once while I was on guard duty at the barracks, walking outside, I became feverish and had to get another marine to finish my watch. I went to a corpsman on duty, and he gave me some pills. He said he would send me to the hospital, but that I would be better off at the barracks. Well, I had the stove stoked up higher, and put all the cover, blankets, overcoats, and anything I could find on the cot. One of my fellow marine roommates had a bottle of vodka under his cot. He said, "Homer, take a few swigs of this. It should do the trick." After a few swigs, I got under all the cover on the cot and started to sweat. Shortly, I fell fast asleep and slept soundly all night. It was a pleasant surprise to wake up the next morning with the fever gone and feeling fine.

Once I caught duty on a truck that was being loaded with boxes of beer by Japanese soldiers. I won't use the word *prisoners* because their officers were managing them until they could be sent back to Japan. Their cooperation was fantastic. They had on nice warm, clean uniforms. They looked healthy and well fed as I observed them from the top of a stack of beer on the truck. They seemed to be almost jolly as they talked among themselves. I wondered what they were talking about. I supposed they had been told that they would be going home in the near future. It was our job to get them there.

I talked to a Chinese tailor, who had shaped up a couple of baggy shirts for me, about the economy. He said the economy was better when the Japanese were in charge. I could understand this because a change in power always causes some disruption. I asked him who would be better for the economy, the Nationalists or the Communists. He did not want to talk about it. I believe the Chinese people liked the marines. The British thought the marines were not dignified enough toward the Chinese. The Russian lady who sold me the pearls said the British knew how to treat the Chinese. The British managed the railroads and the coal mines. The Chinese in the north were of a more ruddy complexion than the Chinese in the south. They seemed to be healthy and well fed, even with their meager food supplies. I did see wheat fields that had been harvested.

One time I took a Chinese girl to a movie. The sound was in English, but the words were written in Chinese at the bottom of the screen. We went in just after the movie was over when the theater was almost empty. You could smell garlic very strongly. The Chinese girl ordered two glasses of hot tea, just as the second show was to start. I had never had hot tea before. It was always iced tea at home. I got to liking the hot tea.

Another time a marine had a Chinese girl arrange for us to visit a Chinese home where there was to be a private party with four Chinese girls who would entertain four of us marines. The Chinese girls would not walk with you on the street. It was against their custom. This particular girl walked ahead alone. We marines walked behind several paces. When we got to the house, a Chinese man invited us inside. There were four Chinese girls there. I never knew what their intent was. It seemed the girls were there for conversation and entertainment. I believed they were a respectable family. Things were going along all right, and the girls could speak some English. The Chinese lead a quiet and polite existence, but we marines were not use to their customs. We got to talking and laughing a little too loud for them, and they asked us to tone down our talk. We apparently did not quiet down enough, because we were asked to leave. The girl who guided us there said she was sorry, but we had to go. She said we made too much noise. I believe these people wanted to keep the respect of their neighbors.

The 15,000 Europeans and white Russians (non-Communist) did not interact socially much with the Chinese. One time three of us marines took three Chinese girls to a restaurant and I overheard one lady of non-Chinese descent say that the marines, speaking of us, should not bring the Chinese girls there, but we ignored the comment.

The USO finally came to China on the urging of the top commanding officer in North China. I went there a couple of times. The first time I heard the song "Sentimental Journey" was at this USO. The song was so popular because many of us would be taking that sentimental journey home in the not-too-distant future. What a sentimental journey it later turned out to be! A tall striking American girl sang the song accompanied by a small band. The band also played dance tunes for us. There were several nationalities of girls who danced with the marines. I asked one, a German Jewish girl, to dance and she accepted. It was not long until another marine cut in. I had told her I was a hillbilly from Arkansas, even though I was from the delta. She said she had heard the expression before. I would have liked to have gotten better acquainted with her.

Soon it was Christmastime and we had a great meal of turkey and dressing. The thing that I will always remember was that at the end of the serving line a young second lieutenant served eggnog to each marine. This was one great gesture of Christmas cheer. I had never seen an officer do this. We were a long way from home, and I know it made everyone feel better. Most of the older officers had been sent back to the States.

The First ASCO was being broken up to some extent. The telephone men were being sent out as replacements for older marines leaving for the States. Several of us were sent down to the railroad station to catch a train going north to the outlying Tangshan and Chanwangtao Marine Headquarters. The marines had a platoon stationed at each railroad bridge to keep the Communists from blowing the bridges up. This was to make sure railway traffic was not interrupted. When we arrived at the railroad station, there were no NCOs around to see that we got on the train. I have never seen such confusion in my life. There was the old locomotive connected to the line up of railroad coaches which looked like coaches from the 1880s. There were about two hundred marine replacements trying to get aboard the coaches with all their gear and seabags. The locomotive had begun to move the coaches, and not near all the marines were aboard. With my carbine in hand, I trotted quickly back to the locomotive that was pushing the the cars. When I reached the end of the cars I held my hand up for the Chinese engineer to stop the train and pointed my carbine at him. He stopped the locomotive. The marines who had not got on the train began trying to get their gear on the coaches. One or two of the new recruits were almost crying, but not the old salts. After a bit almost all were aboard, so I walked back and threw my gear on an outside platform. There were still two or three marines trying to get aboard. They made it as the switch engine pushed the coaches out on the main line. There the coaches were connected to a coal-fired steam locomotive that looked like an American 1920s locomotive. I could hardly believe the large number of Chinese men and children who got on the train. They were riding the platforms on the outside of the coaches. The kids were orphans riding from town to town trying to find some help. The coaches were of all-wood construction except the undercarriage. The benches on each side of the aisle were wooden, something like a smooth church pew. The benches were arranged back to back with the passengers on each bench facing the passengers on the opposite bench.

As we left Tientsin, I began to notice all the telephone poles had been chopped down. I discovered later that our only link to Tientsin was by radio. The Communists were trying to sabotage the infrastructure of the ruling party of Chiang Kai-shek. At times the trains would be fired on by the Communists. To my knowledge, we were not fired on during this trip. Most of the trains would have Chinese Nationalist troops riding the flat cars. I don't recall any Nationalists on this train. That may have been the reason we were not fired on. The two hundred marines aboard may have been some deterrent, also. Two hundred rifles could put out a powerful counter return fire. This train traveled very slowly, only about fifteen miles an hour, and would stop at every small town along the way. At each stop I would observe the people who came out to see the train. Some had business but most were merely curious It was dusk dark when we reached Tangshan, which was about fifty miles north east of Tientsin. We got off the train and walked to the headquarters of the Third Battalion Seventh Marines, where we were expecting to eat supper. When we got there, they had just finished the evening meal, and the cooks would not fix us anything. Unfortunately, we did not have lunch on the train, except maybe a chocolate bar. I can't recall them brewing any more coffee. I think we drank what coffee that was leftover from the evening meal.

We were very upset as we headed back to the cold cars to spend the night. They would not even give us a place to spend the night. Maybe they did not have the room. I guess a bunch of replacements pull about the least weight of anyone in the service. One of my best buddies was one of the replacements. His name was Elliphenson. We placed our seabags on the floor between the seats. We each had two blankets and an overcoat. We placed two blankets over the seabags and used the other two blankets and our overcoats to cover up with. We slept in our dungarees. There was no heat in the car. Even so, we did not get cold during the night. I can't imagine how the poor orphans survived. I don't know what they had to eat, maybe nothing. I don't know what was provided for them. I suppose they huddled together like a covey of birds to stay warm. I judge it was around 15 degrees F. outside, maybe lower in North China in January. I was told that in China if you had family, you were not too bad off. If you were poor and without family you were in trouble. The Chinese were great about taking care of their families.

I believe we did get breakfast the next morning before leaving Tangshan at about 8:00. We reached Peitaiho about 2:00 P.M. This was the headquarters of the Seventh Marine Regiment. Peitaiho was formally a resort center for tourists. It had a nice beach that could be used in the summer. We were sent there to get our assignments to the other battalions that had need of telephone men. The other marine replacements were mostly riflemen and maybe a few headquarters personnel.

Several of the marines were upset about the orphan situation. We talked about it and agonized some about it. I don't know if the towns had any shelter or food for these kids. I vaguely remember them staying inside the railway depot. One instance I remember on our car. There were several Chinese men riding on the platform outside the car. I remember a young girl there, too, who seemed to be alone, but her clothes were not ragged. Someone said, "Why don't we get her to come inside where it is warmer?" The door was opened and one of the marines motioned her to come inside. She hesitated at first but finally came inside. Someone gave her a chocolate bar. She seemed pleased about this and did not seem to be afraid. Naturally, no marine would have harmed her. If anyone had they would have had trouble from the other marines.

I stayed at Peitaiho about three days. Another marine, Charles Hanson from the First ASCO, and I were sent right back to Tangshan where we had stopped off the first night on the train. Charles was from Mitchell, South Dakota. I knew him from the First ASCO, but we became closer friends since we were the only ones at Tangshan from our old outfit. He sent me a Christmas card that first year at home in 1946. He called me his "China Buddy." I tried to look him up years later, when I lived near Sioux City, Iowa. I visited Mitchell, South Dakota, several times trying to locate him but with no success. Hanson was probably the best athlete in the First ASCO. I had known Hanson since naval gunfire training at the Coronado Naval Station near San Diego. He told me he had gone to a small private Bible school near his home town. He was their best football running back. He was a well-built fellow, weighing about one hundred eighty pounds and standing five feet eleven inches tall. I wish we could have had him on our football team back in Arkansas.

When we got back to Tangshan, I mentioned the dirty deal we had gotten by not getting an evening meal. We were able to shower every day, because our barracks had shower facilities. A Chinese barber would do a shave for five cents. Hanson and I were put on telephone switchboard watch, each for only four hours a day. Our link to Tientsin was by radio. We had two lines to the English management establishments. I would listen in on their English accent for fun, not to snoop. They were connected with the coal mines, and I remember them discussing a birthday present for one of their children. I believe they had been there all during the war.

One day at Tangshan, I got to talking to a marine rifleman who had been on duty out on the railroad bridges with one of the platoons placed there to protect the bridges from being blown up by the Communists. This marine platoon had the usual machine guns, bars, rifles, and mortars. One night, as he told it, word came through that a thousand Chinese Communists were nearby. It seems they were only traveling through the area, but did not try to attack. These Communists probably had orders not to attack the marines. They would wait till the marines left China. With only a sixty-man platoon, the Communists might have been able to overrun the platoon. The marine said he was very scared out there.

The Fifth Marines were stationed in the Peiping area, the First Marines in the Tientsen area, with the Seventh Marines in the north at Tangshan, Peitaiho, and Chinwangtao. The Eleventh Marine Artillery was in the Tientsin area. All the railroads were kept secure by the First Marine Division. All these regiments were part of the First Marine Division.

At this stage marines were being sent back to the States so they could reenlist or be discharged. My points were only forty-six, but this was enough that I was getting close to having enough to be sent home. I never went on liberty in Tangshan. All I had on my mind was going home. Some of the marines went on liberty. At Tangshan I was quartered in a large room with about forty other marines. One day we were listening to a marine radio station news report that Tangshan had been surrounded by the Communists. We all looked at each other in disbelief. Someone said, "I just saw a bunch of Nationalists in town." We later found there was a mixup and it was not our Tangshan location. Nevertheless, it was not a comfortable feeling.

There were a bunch of raw replacement marines coming in who would be getting ready to take over our duties. I knew it would not be long before we went home. It was a great feeling, but sort of sad to know we probably would never see one another again. Some of our First ASCO group at Tientsin would call us and ask about the fellows up our way. This was when I was on the switchboard, standing watch. Hein and Klein in our gunfire team had already left, since they had more points than I did.

One day I was on the telephone switchboard and there were three or four marines around shooting the breeze when just outside someone had set off a string of firecrackers. The fellows laughed as I jumped, a reaction leftover from combat. I had a reaction like this for several years after the war. A lot of men who have been under heavy artillery fire have this type of reaction. Even one of our captains in the Third Battalion who had been in all the battles from Guadalcanal to Okinawa, one of the bravest, would be startled and jump whenever he heard any gunfire-type noise.

Near the end of February, Hanson and I received word to get down to Tientsin so we could get ready to board a ship for the States. Our time had come to make the voyage home. I remember waiting at the Tangshan rail station for the train to arrive. Soon the train arrived and we finally got aboard for the trip to Tientsin. After arriving at Tientsin, we stayed at our original barracks for about three days. One of the marines had a .45 automatic his dad had let him have. We were told not to take any weapons with us. I felt sorry for him, because he left it on a shelf in the barracks. I believe I would have tried to sneak it through. It would have been a little difficult because at San Diego we had to have all our gear laid out for final inspection on a cot. He could have shipped it home if he had done it a week earlier.

We assembled together and rode by truck down to the dock where we were placed on a shallow draft landing craft, an LCT as I remember. The craft took us down the river to the coast, where it carried us a few miles out to sea to a troop transport. As land faded from view, with only a sliver in sight, I looked back almost sadly to the fading shoreline and thought to myself, "It will be a long time, if ever, before I see China again. China duty wasn't bad." Shortly we reached the troop ship. It was riding high in the ocean water because it was lightly loaded. I believe we climbed up nets to get aboard the ship, but my memory has faded some on this detail. Our seabags had been tagged and were loaded separately. Word went out that volunteers were needed for mess duty. We would have some benefits of not having to wait in line to eat. Also, we could eat all the leftovers we wanted. I volunteered because I wanted to gain a little weight so I would look better when I got home. I still had not gained all my weight back from eating dehydrated food and Spam, although we did eat some better in China. I still had time to get out on deck after completing mess duty. We sailed into Tokyo Bay for a two-day stay. I don't know why, maybe to pick up more troops or supplies. I could see snow-covered Mount Fuji out to the northwest of Tokyo. It was so strange, just like I was looking at a picture instead of the real mountaintop. It was one of those things you are not looking for and suddenly there it is, big as life. It would take us about three weeks to reach San Diego.

I had a friend in the First ASCO, Proctor from California, who served with another battalion in the First Marine Division. I always considered myself part of the First Marine Division even though the First ASCO was only attached to the division. In the evenings after finishing mess duty, cleaning the huge pots and other cooking vessels, Proctor and I went out on the deck at the bow of the ship and talked about our dreams of the future. Proctor talked about his dad's involvement with a small mining operation in California. I talked about going off to college and maybe becoming an electrical engineer. For me, this did come to pass.

At times, the ship ran into some tall waves. I was concerned because the ship rode so high in the water. It would roll from side to side almost dipping water. I don't remember any bad storms, but the Pacific was rough in March. I stayed on deck a lot when not doing mess duty. I received a heavy tan from the sun rays. I did not get seasick on the trip across the Pacific. In fact, the trip was uneventful. With not much else to do, many marines played cards. I could hardly believe it when we finally sailed into the harbor at San Diego. We had just finished the noon meal when word came that we would be leaving the ship shortly to go over to the marine base to get discharged. My mess duty pals and I were not interested in finishing the cleaning of the cooking vessels. Marines were beginning to disembark. We did not stay to clean the vessels, even though one of the navy chief cooks said we had to clean up the kitchen before we left. I didn't want to miss the special busses waiting to take us over to the marine base. We were taken back to the same huts we were housed in during boot camp.

While in the chow line, I recognized one of my old boot camp friends. We talked some about where we had been since boot camp. It was a great feeling to be back. I was still only twenty years old. But I was now a grown man and would be twenty-one in four months. I had been around men only, except for a few Chinese girls. Women's voices sounded different and high pitched. I went to the base theater that evening where I had seen some movies in boot camp and some bands with celebrity women singers. It took about three days to get discharged. We got a final physical, and we were sent down to a warehouse to get a full complement of clothes we might have been lacking. I got a new pair of shoes, a khaki shirt, and a set of dungarees as I remember. Then we had a final inspection with all our clothes laid neatly on our cots. We were given a final check and enough money to buy a ticket home. A young lieutenant gave us a going-away speech and wished us well. He thanked us for our service to our country, representing the U.S. Marine Corps and our country. I thought it was a fine gesture for our service. We had been given the opportunity to enlist at our new rank. I was promoted to corporal. I was surprised when one of my friends from the First ASCO did reenlist. I was also surprised that he was listed as a PFC on his address sent me in 1949 on a list of two hundred former marines from the First ASCO.

Our seabags were shipped home separately, so after getting my corporal strips sewed onto my uniform and my khaki shirt and picking up ribbons that I had earned the right to wear, I was ready to catch the next train home. I don't remember much about the train ride to Arkansas, except that I stopped off at El Paso, Texas, to get a haircut and a shave. I remember the temperature was very warm. Everyone treated me with respect, a far different cry from how our Vietnam veterans were treated later on. I remember one marine I knew getting off in Marshall, Texas. He looked out the window and said, "There my folks are on the platform waiting for me." I quickly said goodbye to him as he hurried to greet them. The train made only a quick stop. We reached Little Rock, Arkansas, that day. I spent the night in Little Rock and caught a bus early the next morning to Forrest City. From there I caught a bus going to Helena, which was twenty miles east of Marvell. I got off the bus at Barton, which was eight miles east of Marvell. There I waited for the old Brocato Bus Line that served all the towns along the way to Brinkley, Arkansas. When this bus arrived, I paid for the trip to Marvell. When I got on the bus, I went back to the rear of the bus where the blacks rode, and I sat down there as a gesture of good will. One or two whites did kind of stare at me. Since I had been through far worse than stares on Okinawa, it did not bother me. Soon the bus pulled into Marvell, my home town with a population of 1,820, which served many more people out in the surrounding countryside. The average farm then was about eighty acres. Today it is about twelve hundred acres. The largest farms are seven thousand acres or more.

I walked around looking for a ride to my folks' home, four miles north of town. At that time there were two main dry goods stores, Hirsch's and Davidson's. These were owned by Jewish families. They were also cotton buyers. Out behind Hirsch's store was a large open lot where many of the small cotton farmers would leave their wagons and teams while they did their trading for groceries and supplies. This was during the '20s, '30s, and '40s. Things had not changed much except now fewer people went to town in wagons. One of the local salesmen saw me and asked if I would like a ride home. I said yes. He said, "Let me get the car and I will run you out to your folks' place."

Soon he pulled up to the small bridge at my folks' driveway. I got out, and he backed his car up and headed back to Marvell. With my small satchel in hand I started up the driveway to the house. Dad and Mom happened to be in the yard near the house. They saw me and started running to meet me, and I started running, too. I judge it was about 2:00 P.M. Dad was fifty-three and Mom was forty-three. I had not seen them in two and a half years because I never got a furlough home. By the way, the Marine Corps did pay me later for the furlough time they owed me, $170. Mom was crying as she hugged me. Dad hugged me, too. We walked back to the house, went inside, and sat down at the breakfast table in the kitchen. It was a warm day and a warm welcome that April 1, 1946. Sitting there, I was just overcome with emotion. I said, "Dad, I can't believe I am home. It will take me a few minutes for it all to sink in." The best way I could explain it is like maybe being released from prison. I didn't have to answer to

Homer Grantham was discharged on March 29, 1946. Here he is ready to catch the train to Arkansas on this rather windy day.

any NCOs. I had charge of my life. (Recently I drove by the old place. The old house and barn were gone, but the memory of the scene of me running to meet my folks with the old house and barn in the background lives on in my memory.)

Dad said, "Son, I want to show you something." We walked into the bedroom, where my two-and-a-half-year-old brother was asleep on the bed. He was born about a week after I had left for San Diego. Later my three sisters came in from school. It was great to see them, too. Robert, my brother, twenty-two months younger than I, was over at Henderson State College at Arkadelphia, Arkansas. I would see him in a week or so. Late that afternoon we rode up to where my two uncles lived to see them and my cousins. I left my uniform on so they could see me in it because it was the first and last time they would see me in my marine uniform.

EPILOGUE

What does the past mean to us today? That is the question that I want to consider. While serving in the U.S. Marine Corps I believed this country of ours was worth fighting for. Our way of life was being threatened, and I felt that duty was calling me to respond. Of course, the excitement of being involved in this effort played a big part of my World War II marine experience, a time that has meant much to me since then. I liked the camaraderie and fun I had being associated with many of my fellow marines. It was just a wonderful experience.

There were some sad times, and I lost some good friends whom I have never forgotten. Some gave the ultimate sacrifice, which I have come to appreciate more as I have grown older. There were some who suffered more than others and they carry the scars to this day. Many have gone on to that great beyond where we will meet again some glad day. I recently looked up the meaning of the expression, *Semper Fidelis*. It still means *always faithful*. Often I think of all my old buddies. I am always faithful in that respect.

Faith in God, country, friends, neighbors, and our form of government is so important to me. This great experience in our Republic has given us freedom to enrich our lives. I invested two and a half years for it in the marines, so you might say I have a vested interest to see that our country does well. My wish is to see all the people in government look out for our interests and protect our form of government. The only way to do this is to keep an educated and enlightened people who will elect the right people and keep good government. Each generation will have to exert its best efforts to keep it that way. We could lose it all in just one or two generations.

While in the marines I learned to respect those in authority and to carry out my duties and responsibilities. In fact, I learned to be a good citizen. I had respect for my fellow marines and tried to treat them as I wanted to be treated. The training and experience gained in the marines has stood me well down through the years. The ability to stick it out helped me get through engineering school. I moved around a lot in the first ten years after earning my engineering degree. I never lost faith in myself and finally landed some good jobs that I stuck with and was successful at.

What does the future hold for the younger generation and also for future generations? In the marines we were taught to be self-reliant, flexible, and innovative, and to persevere under tough circumstances. I believe the other armed forces taught this also. This is one of the reasons we won World War II. If we will continue with this same attitude, I believe we will always have a great country. America has enormous resources: its roads, railways, riverways, utilities such as electrical, telephone, water, and sewage, farms, factories, timber, computer networks. I could go on and on. Not least of all are our health facilities, which are the best in the world. However, our greatest resource is our people, young and old. I know our educational system is the best in the world overall. The only thing that could be lacking is the ability of our young people to take advantage of the opportunities available to them. We are in an age where the best education possible is needed. An uneducated people cannot remain free. Look about the world and you can see it is true.

Our western culture got us where we are, and with our abundance we've become the envy of the world. Trust in a benevolent God is not to be overlooked. I believe the Lord has blessed us as a nation. We have not been perfect but have strived to correct wrongs. I hope we can teach our young people not to expect to survive by handouts but to work hard and with wisdom to secure the great American dream. One way to help is be a knowledgeable voter and to vote one's convictions. Remember that the government has only what we allow it to have. Good government is a wonderful resource when it is kept restrained to its needful duties and does not invade our lives unnecessarily and try to do for us what we can do better ourselves.

We can be held down by too many laws and regulations. There should be enough laws and regulations to provide each person a fair playing field in his pursuit of livelihood and happiness. We should be thankful for our religious freedom. The trend to restrict this should be changed. We should be allowed to practice our religion as our conscience dictates.

Yes, I believe the people lucky enough to live in American will have a great future if we honor our Judeo-Christian heritage. This, again, got us where we are today and will help ensure a great future for our country and our people.

Remember that the world has always been a dangerous place. We cannot be naive and let our guard down. We must remain strong and be able to defend our liberties and the country that ensures those liberties. We should be careful about other ideologies that some would foster on us. We need to hang on to what we think of as the "good old American way." I will not attempt to explain it, but I love it.

APPENDIX

Earlier I did not intend to tell about the Fifth, Seventh, and Eleventh Marine Regiments, only my gunfire team's part. However, since most of the ones who read this account will not read the other accounts, to do justice to these three regiments and to the marines who fought with them, they need to be recognized for what they accomplished. Credit needs to be given to the Eighty-first Army Division, since they did the final elimination of the last pockets of Japanese left on Peleliu.

In September 1944, in Peleliu, the Eighty-first Army's 321st Regiment relieved the First Marine Regiment, while the Fifth Marine's Third Battalion swung around from the east side of Peleliu to the west side and proceeded where the Third Battalion First Marines had left off. The Eighty-first had made some advances up the west road. The 3/5* battalion moved through the 321 Regiment of the Eighty-first Division and proceeded to the north end of Peleliu with considerable action taking place. The Seventh Marines had stayed on the south portion of Bloodynose Ridge to keep the Japanese trapped within a U shape around the ridge.

In one area the 321st Regiment made good progress up the west road, but 3/7 had fallen behind due to the slower progress up on the ridges more heavily defended, with greater resistance being met. Part of the army's 3/321 was sent to fill the gap. The Japanese hit them hard, and they fell back to stay in contact with

---

*3/5: Third Battalion, Fifth Marines; 3/321: Third Battalion, 321st Regiment; 2/7: Second Battalion, Seventh Marines; 3/7: Third Battalion, Seventh Marines.

the balance of 3/321. The Seventh realized a gap had developed and sent their I Company to retake the ridge that 3/321 had vacated. The commanding officer of 3/7 was concerned that the Japanese might pour through this gap. The next day, 3/321 made better progress. The Seventh Regiment continued to probe into the ridges but remained rather static until the 3/5 could finish the taking of Ngesebus Island that joined Peleliu by a causeway.

The attack on Ngesebus was one of the most successful beach assaults in the war. One battleship and two cruisers opened fire at 0800. At twenty minutes to H-hour naval shelling stopped, and the marine Corsairs started their bombing and strafing runs. Led by thirteen amphibious tanks in the first wave at 9:05 followed by the second wave of 3/5, which hit the beach with not much resistance, on the September 28. After considerable action, 3/5 finished the island assault on the twenty-ninth. Now 3/5 moved back to the north end of Peleliu with elements of the army's 321 taking over that island's defenses.

All this time the Seventh and the balance of the Fifth Marines held the Japanese in check, with the other two battalions of the Fifth continuing to eliminate the Japanese on the northern ridges. On September 29 the resistance on the northernmost portion virtually came to an end.

I would like to say something about the Eleventh Marine Artillery Regiment. They worked very hard to fill their part of the assault and were some of the last to leave Peleliu. Without the artillery the taking of the island would have been in doubt. This is my opinion. Of course the infantrymen get most of the attention, as they should. The Eleventh had spotters to call in the artillery barrages at or near the front lines just as naval gunfire spotters did for naval gunfire. (I'll never forget the feeling of hearing the time-on-target of those terrific barrages going over and the sound as all the shells landed in one great crescendo on Okinawa.) The artillery had to be very careful and keep close communication with the companies on the front lines to prevent shells from falling in on friendly troops. Many times the Eleventh brought 75s up near the front to deliver point-blank fire on Peleliu. Artillery was placed to lay down calibrated nonstop barrages anywhere on the island. Their combined firepower was nearly 150 pieces, including forty 155 mm "Long Toms" and the other 75s and 105s. The marine artillerymen fired 133,000 rounds of shells in thirty-five days.

Naval gunfire was used heavily on Peleliu. Our Fourth JASCO team, with 3/1 of the First Regiment, called in and directed 11,000 rounds from destroyers with cruisers and one battleship during eight days of action. On the first day, help came at a critical time. At that time there was no artillery available, only what our gunfire spotting teams could call in from the navy destroyers, cruisers, and battleships.

Many rear-echelon came up to help as stretcher bearers. This included the Second Marine Air Wing. The Fourth JASCO was assigned to fill in as stretcher bearers. I talked to several on Pavuvu about their experience, with them saying it was very hazardous. Some were wounded.

On September 30 General William H. Rupertus assigned the Seventh Regiment's badly depleted forces to begin the assault on the Umurbrogol pocket. Even though the gains looked promising, there was evidence that the battalions could not sustain the attack for long. On October 1, 3/5 relieved 2/7 along the southwestern perimeter of the Umurbrogol. On October 3, in a coordinated attack, the 2/7 was to attack northward to seize Walt Ridge, and the 3/7 was to attack southward to take Boyd Ridge. At the same time 3/5 was to attack the Five Sisters Ridges in the southern portion of the pocket. After very fierce fighting, Walt Ridge and Boyd Ridge were taken. The weather turned unfavorable on the third and continued through the fourth.

For the first time the East Road was open for supply and

Tanks and infantry assault Jap positions on a Peleliu ridge. *USMC photo, courtesy Nimitz Museum.*

Marines fire their weapons and throw hand grenades at the Japs in the caves and on the hillside. *USMC photo, courtesy Nimitz Museum.*

evacuation, although the Japanese interfered some from positions in the Horseshoe, in the draw between the Walt and Boyd Ridges. At this point an attempt was made to take Hill 120 by 3/7. Company L had taken the three knobs, and Major Hurst decided to press on and seize Hill 120. Just when it appeared Hill 120 had been captured, the platoon on this ridge began to draw fire and suffered several casualties. They got trapped and could not escape from Japanese fire. Only a few men made it out. There were only eleven men left out of forty-eight who had ascended the ridge, of these only five emerged unscathed. The Seventh was so weakened that General Rupertus decided to have the Fifth Marines relieve them. The relief took place on October 5 and 6.

For the Seventh Marines, all major combat was over. The Fifth Marines were given the responsibility for the final drive into the Umurbrogol with the continuation of heavy combat. Colonel Harold "Bucky" Harris, commander, Fifth Marines, decided to use a different approach for the conquest of the Umurbrogol ridges. Using a slower and deliberate approach did not meet with approval from division headquarters. They went on to take Baldy Ridge and Hill 140 even with heavy resistance from the Japanese. One of the last innovations was to disassemble a 75 mm howitzer, take it to the top of Hill 140, and reassemble it behind a layer of sand bags, all of which had to be manhandled all the way to the top of the ridge. The howitzer fired eleven rounds into a cave with good effect. A second howitzer was placed in position along the southeastern perimeter of Walt Ridge. It was able to fire directly at the Five Sisters and the China Wall.

On the morning of October 13, 3/5 was the only unit in the line with an offensive mission. The Japanese did infiltrate to take Hill 140, but were repulsed. On October 13, Colonel Kunio Nakagawa reported his total strength was 1,150 military, including naval personnel with an arsenal of 13 machine guns, 500 rifles with 20,000 rounds of ammunition, 12 grenade dischargers with

150 rounds, one 20 mm automatic gun with 50 rounds, one anti-tank gun with 350 rounds, a 70 mm howitzer with 120 rounds, 1,300 grenades, and 40 anti-tank mines. Yes, the elimination of the final pockets of the resistance would be difficult.

The days of the First Marine Division on Peleliu were numbered. The last full day of combat for the Fifth Marines in the Umurbrogol pocket began with an air strike against the Five Sisters.

After a mortar barrage, I Company attacked the western portion of the pocket. There was heavy crossfire from the Japanese but by late afternoon a gain of 250 yards was made. The company had reached a point abreast of the northernmost point of two of the Five Brothers and about 200 yards west of the China Wall. The marines established a perimeter for the night.

While Company I was advancing south, Company C of 1/7 was advancing against the southern Japanese defense line, having been attached to the Fifth Marines. They gained 125 yards, and the advance came to a stop. As a result of this action by 3/5 and 1/7, the western part of the pocket was reduced by about 400 yards. The Umurbrogol pocket was reduced to an area of about 400 yards by 500 yards. With only small skirmishes elsewhere on Peleliu, the action by the First Marine Division ended on October 14.

According to figures up to October 20, 1944, the First Marine Division had taken the heavily fortified and defended island from the Japanese. They had sustained a total of 6,265 casualties, a total of 1,124 marines killed in action and dead from wounds, 5,024 were wounded in action, and 177 were missing. The final chapter was yet to be written by the Eighty-first Army Division.

Major General Mueller, CO of the Eighty-first Infantry Division, took charge of final operations on Peleliu on October 20. On this date he took over the last elements of the First Marine Division still on the island. He commanded the 321st Regiment and the 1/321, which had returned from Ulithi, the 710th Tank Battalion, and elements of the 154th Engineer Battalion.

FINAL 81ST INFDIV OPERATIONS

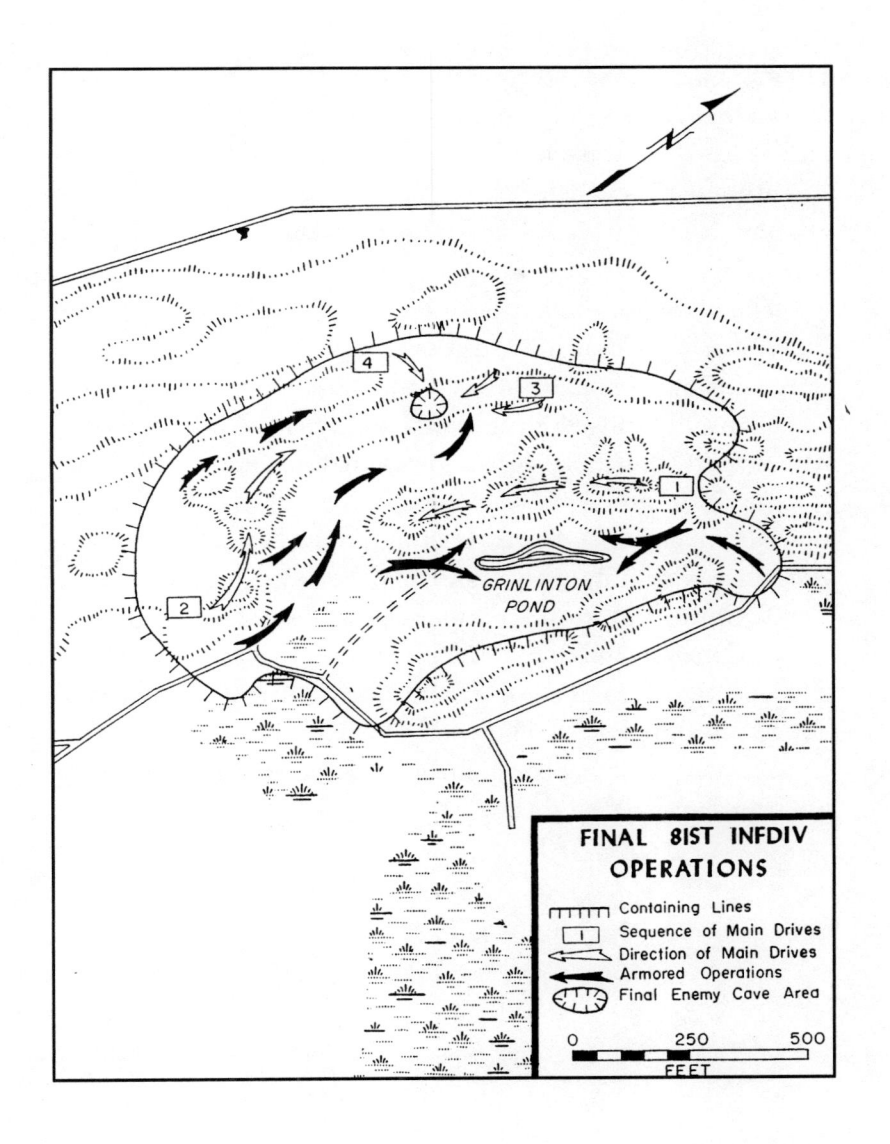

- Containing Lines
- Sequence of Main Drives
- Direction of Main Drives
- Armored Operations
- Final Enemy Cave Area

From the time the 321st Regiment had relieved the First Marines on September 23, the 321st had lost 98 men killed and 468 wounded, while killing more than 1,500 Japanese and capturing 108.

General Mueller's plan closely resembled Colonel Harris's

APPENDIX 137

tactics. This was to slowly and methodically tighten the grip around the pocket with a minimum loss of life. Using the 321st and 323rd Regiments, the Eighty-first proceeded to wipe out the last of the Japanese defenders. The fighting was just as fierce as any the marines had experienced. Air support and artillery was used extensively. The Japanese resisted for every foot of the pocket.

The battle for the last Japanese pocket on Peleliu began on November 22. Colonel Nakagawa reported that an enemy force was attacking with flamethrowers and his men were on the verge of collapse. During the night of November 24, both General Murai and Colonel Nakagawa committed suicide.

On the morning of November 25, eight rifle companies cautiously converged on the center of the China Wall. There was no resistance with only silence greeting the advancing solders. At 1100, Colonel Watson, commander of the 323rd Regiment, reported that organized resistance had come to an end on Peleliu. The enemy had fulfilled his commitment to fight to the death. There was some scattered individual harassment that followed by Japanese who had escaped annihilation, but these were soon either killed or captured.

BIBLIOGRAPHY

The books listed below are references that I consulted for checking facts and dates used in my story. I made some references to George P. Hunt's book, *Coral Comes High,* because my commanding officer, Lieutenant Monk Myers, was in Hunt's general area during the first two days of the battle on Peleliu. Monk carried the message from Lieutenant Colonel Sabol to Hunt that first evening, winning the Silver Star Medal. There were references made about the gallant stand Hunt's Company K made the first two nights when the Japanense attacked with such great fury. For the Appendix, I garnered the facts on the actions of the Fifth, Seventh, and Eleventh Marine Regiments and the Eighty-first Army, along with the maps from the History of Marine Corps Operations. My story is about what I saw, as I remember it, filtered by the passage of time.

Falk, Standley. *Bloodiest Victory: Palaus.* New York: Ballantine Books, 1974.
Frank, Benis M., and Henry I. Shaw Jr. *Victory and Occupation: History of Marine Corps Operations in World War II.* Vol. 5. Washington, D.C.: Historical Branch, G-3 Division, Headquarters, U.S. Marine Corps, 1968.
Garand, George W., and Truman R. Strobridge. *Western Pacific Operations: History of Marine Corps Operations in World War II.* Vol. 4. Washington, D.C.: Historical Division, HQMC, 1971.
Hough, Maj. Frank O. *The Assault on Peleliu.* Washington, D.C.: Historical Division, HQMC, 1950.
Hunt, George P. *Coral Comes High.* New York: Harper and Brothers, 1946.
Sledge, E. B. *With the Old Breed at Peleliu and Okinawa.* New York: Oxford University Press, 1990.